I0566110

ENCEPHALON

by Kerry Marie Sloan
&
Dan Yager

STARGAZER BOOKS
Philadelphia

STARGAZER
BOOKS

Copyright © 2018 STARGAZER BOOKS LLC

All rights reserved. This book or any portion thereof
may not be reproduced or used in any manner whatsoever
without the express written permission of the publisher
except for the use of brief quotations in a book review.

This STARGAZER BOOKS paperback edition September 2018

STARGAZER BOOKS and the STARGAZER BOOKS logo
are trademarks of STARGAZER BOOKS LLC.

For information about special discounts for bulk purchases,
book signings, and talks by the authors please contact

Special Events - Stargazer Books
info@stargazerbooks.com
or visit our website
www.stargazerbooks.com

Edited by Linda Sloan
Design by Dan Yager

Manufactured in the United States of America

Library of Congress Control Number: 2018955591

ISBN-13: 978-1-944523-06-0
ISBN-10: 1-944523-06-5

To strong females.

CONTENTS

00000001

MALVERN

"That concludes our virtual tour of the computer science department," said Jane. "Thank you for your interest in Malvern University. We hope you consider applying, and we look forward to welcoming you as new students in the future."

Jane looked up and focused in on the small group of potential students projected into the virtual classroom. She tried hard not to yawn. It had been a long day, she was tired, and she still had several hours of work to do in the lab.

"I'm going to place the prompter in exchange mode now for a brief question and answer session," said Jane. "Does anyone have any questions?"

There was a long silence and Jane breathed a sigh of relief. She was about to deactivate her Visual Cortex Stimulator and end the session, but, before she could, a question alert popped up in her field of view. Jane tried not to look annoyed. For a brief moment, she toyed with the idea of ignoring the prompt that was blinking irritatingly before her eyes. But she knew she didn't have a choice. Answering questions was one of the most important parts of the virtual tour.

Jane crossed her fingers and hoped that it would be an easy question, maybe something about the dorms or the dining hall that would only take a few minutes to answer.

"Yes," she said, after reluctantly accepting the

prompt.

A tall, scrawny boy appeared in the center of her visual field and looked at Jane expectantly.

"Isn't this the school where RJ Robotics got started?" he asked, eagerly. "Remy and John were students here, weren't they?"

Jane blanched. Of course, she should have expected this question. The famous robotics company was Malvern's major claim to fame. But RJ Robotics wasn't something she wanted to talk about, especially not today.

"Yes," said Jane, shortly. "About five years ago, Remy Crofton and John Westin, two of Malvern's computer science students, founded RJ Robotics. They designed their first robot here."

"So your robotics program must be really good," said the boy excitedly. "RJ Robotics is the biggest robotics company in the world!"

"The robotics program is good," answered Jane slowly, "but it's still only a small part of the computer science department. We've been working on expanding the entire department over the past few years with grant money and..."

The boy interrupted Jane, "I heard that RJ Robotics wanted to give the department money, but that their offer was turned down. Is that true?"

Jane tried not to let the surprise show on her face. RJ Robotics attempted involvement with the school was supposed to be confidential.

"I'm not at liberty to discuss that," said Jane, trying to keep her voice calm "but I do know that the computer science department is committed to maintaining its independence and integrity. Any money that we receive has to be used for pure research purposes, not to develop robots in order to increase a company's profits."

The boy rolled his eyes. He looked as if he was

about to ask another question, but, before he could, Jane saw another blinking prompt.

"Yes," said Jane, in relief, as she acknowledged the prompt. "What's your question?"

A petite blond took the place of the scrawny boy and began speaking in a soft voice that Jane had to strain to hear.

"Could you tell us a little bit more about your own research?" she asked. "I've read some of your papers, and I think your work is fascinating."

Jane looked at the girl, pleasantly surprised. Not many people were familiar with her work.

"Well, when I started at Malvern University, I was interested in object oriented programming," explained Jane. "As most of you probably know, these are programs made up of simple subroutines that can be combined in order to complete more complex tasks. I theorized that the brain might work in the same way. If you could figure out the brain's subroutines, you could figure out how the brain works. Over the past few years, my research has progressed very slowly from theory to practice."

"You're working with animals now, right?" asked the girl.

"That's right," said Jane. "My main focus is on healing cognitive brain damage in animals, with the ultimate goal of improving human health. I use a process of non-invasive digital dissection that was developed in this lab. I've spent the last five years mapping the neural brain pathways of several animals. I started small, with a fruit fly. Over time, I've worked my way up, increasing the evolutionary complexity to higher functioning mammals. Currently I'm mapping the brain of a Holland Lop rabbit."

The girl nodded knowingly. "Is it possible to work with you if I'm accepted to Malvern? I'd love to help you with your research."

Jane smiled. "That would be a question for your advisor, but, in general, all of the students in the computer science department are welcome to take part in research. And who knows? You could potentially be the focus of my next digital dissection. If you're evolutionarily close enough to a rabbit, that is."

The students laughed at her joke and Jane sighed in relief. Normally her jokes weren't that well received.

"If there are no more questions..." began Jane, hoping to wrap things up and end the session on a good note.

Before Jane could finish speaking, the scrawny boy was back at the prompter again. Jane reluctantly accepted the prompt, but before she could say anything the boy started talking quickly.

"I've heard that you worked with Remy and John when you were all students at Malvern together. Is it true that they stole your brain research to start their company?" he asked.

Jane paled for a moment and then took a deep breath to regain her composure. How did this boy know about her connection with RJ Robotics?

"Yes," said Jane shortly, "I did work for a brief period with the founders of RJ Robotics. We were all students here at the same time and it was inevitable that our paths would cross. But they certainly didn't steal my research. In the computer industry, ideas are often shared. Some of the technology they've developed has been inspired by my brain research, but they've also made a lot of their own innovations, especially in the pure robotics field."

"So RJ Robotics took your brain research one step further... hacking into the brain to find the right pathways for their technology?" he asked.

"Hacking is a strong word," said Jane. "I'd say it was

4

more like reverse engineering the brain to find the programming hooks where they could insert their own code. And, I wouldn't say that what RJ Robotics did was the next logical step forward. When working with new technologies, there should be a lengthy period of testing. We need to fully understand new technology before we make use of it."

"You think they rushed it," said the boy, rolling his eyes at her. "But the things they've developed are all technologies we depend on today…like the Brain Band! The only reason we can all see each other and interact right now is because we all have Brain Bands. We couldn't live without them! They make life better."

Suddenly, as if on cue, the group of students burst into song. "If you need a helping hand, trust the leading neural brand . . . Brain Band!"

It was an extremely annoying commercial jingle for RJ Robotics, and Jane detested it.

"Alright, alright," said Jane, trying not to sound annoyed. "We get it. We all know how amazing Visual Cortex Stimulators are."

"Brain Bands are amazing!" said the scrawny boy, excitedly. "But that's the point I'm trying to make. The Brain Band is based on your research. Doesn't that make you upset?"

"Not at all," said Jane, calmly. "My work has been used as the starting point for lots of new technologies, not just Visual Cortex Stimulators, or Brain Bands."

"Then why aren't you rich like the founders of RJ Robotics?" demanded the boy. "Isn't that why we're all interested in computer science in the first place?"

A few of the students in the virtual classroom laughed and nodded in agreement.

"A life of service is its own reward," said Jane, firmly "I'm glad that my research has helped people, and I'm also glad that others have found new applications for my ideas. If that results in a company making a profit, I'm happy for them too, as long as everything is done ethically."

Before the scrawny boy could respond, another question prompt began blinking. Jane sighed. This question and answer session was starting to feel like walking through a minefield. Couldn't she just be done for the day?

"This is the last question," said Jane, as she acknowledged the prompt, "and then we'll wrap things up."

A short, disheveled young man took the center of the room. He looked as if he spent most of his time in a dark basement and had only emerged for the virtual tour.

"What about the control algorithm?" asked the boy eagerly, in a high pitched voice. "RJ Robotics started the search for it here! Are you all still looking for it? And who's going to find it first? Do you think they'll beat you to it?"

Jane was appalled. The control algorithm? Where were these students coming up with this stuff?

Jane paused for a moment in order to gather her thoughts. Then she said, dismissively, "The control algorithm doesn't exist. It's an extremely far fetched theory. There's no basis in fact for its existence."

"But if it did exist," pursued the boy, unperturbed by Jane's answer, "and you found it, it would be incredible. With that type of power, you'd be able to control the entire brain!"

"The control algorithm is nonsense!" snapped Jane. "No one is searching for it. That type of research would be pointless. You can't find something that isn't real!"

A few of the students in the group laughed, but the short boy looked at her skeptically. It was clear he didn't believe her.

Before anyone could say anything else, Jane spoke

quickly, "That's it for today. Thank you for your interest and I hope you enjoyed the virtual tour of Malvern University."

As soon as Jane finished her sentence, she deactivated her Visual Cortex Stimulator, or VCS, and pulled it off the back of her head. Immediately, the room was empty. Jane breathed a deep sigh of relief. The session was finally over. What had gotten into these students? It was as if they were trying to give her a nervous breakdown with their questions.

Jane sighed again and rubbed her forehead. She still hadn't gotten used to wearing her Visual Cortex Stimulator. Her boycott of anything related to RJ Robotics made an official Brain Band off limits. This had forced her to cobble together her own VCS from spare pieces and parts in the lab. Surprisingly, based on her limited resources, she had been able to program several improvements into her homemade VCS. But it gave her no comfort knowing that she could outdo RJ Robotics in Brain Band design. She still disliked her VCS, and, no matter what she did, it gave her horrible headaches.

Jane's glance rested on a large screen that was hanging on the wall. Normally it posted announcements and other university related news. However, just as she looked at it, the screen, in bright, garish colors, flashed the logo for RJ Robotics, and the words:

"Malvern University thanks RJ Robotics, the inventors of the Brain Band, for making our virtual classrooms possible."

Jane jumped up and rushed over to the screen. She banged the power button violently until the screen went blank and the RJ Robotics logo disappeared.

"Not today," she muttered angrily to herself, as she gathered up her things and rushed out of the room.

00000010

HARDSCRABBLE

Jane made her way slowly back to the computer science building where her lab and office were located. She felt drained after the difficult question and answer session. She was hoping that the walk across campus would reenergize her.

As Jane neared the computer science building, she reached into her bag for her VCS and put it back on. She'd programmed the security system in her office to interface with it. It was supposed to unlock her office door as she approached, bypassing the more complicated security protocols in the building. Unfortunately, her homemade VCS didn't always function properly and gaining access to her office was sometimes a challenge.

Jane walked up to her office door, crossed her fingers and whispered, "Please work."

She stood there for a few moments, waiting for the door to slide open, but nothing happened. Jane took a deep breath, removed her VCS, and gave it a good shake. Sometimes that helped. She put her VCS back on and held her breath. Suddenly, the door jerked, and then slid open slowly. Jane breathed a sigh of relief. Two tries wasn't that bad.

Jane had intended to spend the afternoon working, but, after answering so many questions about RJ Robotics, she wasn't sure she felt like doing anything.

"Why does it still bother me so much?" Jane

muttered to herself. "It's been five years, shouldn't I be over it by now?"

Jane frowned and her shoulders drooped as she looked around her office. Five long years had gone by, but very little had changed. Jane was a clever programmer, but there was only so much she could do with the outdated technology in the lab. Malvern's equipment was just barely functional, held together with the programmatic equivalent of duct tape and string. She had a vision for a machine that would map neural pathways efficiently, but it was barely in the design stage. Any hope of completing her research thesis within the next century would require a huge influx of capital.

"And there's no chance of that happening, unless I sell my soul to the highest bidder," said Jane to herself, despairingly.

Then, despite herself, she smiled. There, sitting peacefully in a corner of the room, was her pet rabbit. Jane walked over to the rabbit, who was looking at her expectantly.

"You missed me, didn't you?" she asked, as she picked it up.

Jane sat down at her desk, letting the rabbit nestle into her lap. "You always make me feel better," she said, as she gently stroked the small creature.

After a few moments, Jane took a deep breath and readjusted her VCS.

"Alright Bunnykins," she said. "Break time is over. Hopefully I can get something done today."

But, before Jane could get started, she received a ping on her VCS. Someone wanted to audio chat with her privately. The person's identifier was blocked, which was strange. Communications protocol required all VCS interactions to include personal identifiers.

Normally, Jane ignored incoming pings when she was trying to work. Usually it was a colleague in the

10

department who wanted a favor. And Jane always had trouble saying no. But this was different.

"Anyone willing to break the law to talk to me should be interesting," said Jane to herself, as she accepted the communications prompt on her VCS.

"This is Jane Christensen. How can I help you?"

"Hi Jane. It's Remy . . ."

Jane froze and her face paled. She tried to say something, but nothing came out.

"Jane? . . . Are you still there?"

"Yes," whispered Jane finally, "but I don't have anything to say to you. You know where we stand. I'm going to disconnect now."

"Hold on," said Remy, his words coming out in a rush. "Give me a chance. I want to make amends for everything that happened. Let's talk. We'll get everything out in the open."

"No," said Jane, "there's nothing for us to talk about."

"Wait!" replied Remy. "It's not just me. John's in town too. "

"John's with you?" said Jane, her voice softening slightly.

"We're both in town for a new product launch," said Remy. "But that's not what we want to talk about. We have some incredible stuff going on at RJ Robotics and we want you to be a part of it."

"Oh I see," said Jane, shortly. "That's why you're calling. You want something."

"No Jane! It's not like that. I swear. Just one meeting, that's all I'm asking for," pleaded Remy. "It'll be like old times again, you'll see."

"That's what I'm afraid of," said Jane. "I'm not going to see you or John, not now, not ever. Don't try to contact me again."

Jane disconnected and took off her VCS. She looked down at Bunnykins and tried to pet her, but her hands were shaking too violently.

"I'm sorry, Bunnykins," she said, on the verge of tears. "I'm so sorry."

Jane closed her eyes, trying to block out all thoughts of Remy. However, despite her best efforts, her thoughts drifted back to the past.

***

Jane was sitting silently in front of the college review board. One of the school trustees was saying something, but she wasn't listening. All she could do was stare at the text that she had just received on her cell phone.

"I can't face the board with you today. I'm dropping out of school. Please don't hate me. John."

There were three chairs at the table where Jane was sitting, but two of them were empty. Jane hadn't expected Remy to be there, but John...she had been certain that he would show up. But he hadn't, and he wasn't going to. She was completely alone.

The man who had been speaking shuffled some papers on the table before him. "Let me make sure I have this right," he said, as he selected one of the papers to read from.

"You, Remy Crofton, and John Westin were representing Malvern University in the X Prize College Robotics Challenge. Your contest entry involved using a probe to map the neural pathways in the brain. You used your experience and prior research to hypothesize sub-routines that govern animal mobility. Is that correct?"

Jane nodded without looking up.

"During the research process, you got behind, jeopardizing your ability to meet the contest deadline. Rather than admit defeat, you contacted one of the contest judges and offered him a bribe. Then, you tried to speed up your research by scanning animal brains

12

with a machine that hadn't been fully tested, thus killing several laboratory animals."

Jane continued to sit silently.

"These are serious accusations," said the man gravely. "Do you have anything to say for yourself?"

Jane finally looked up at the group of men and women who were there to judge her. All the words of defense that she had prepared were gone. All she could think about were her friends who had betrayed her and the animals that had been killed. Nothing else seemed to matter.

"No," whispered Jane.

"No!" said the man in surprise. "Don't you want to defend yourself? You and your absent friends have been accused of violating our school's animal cruelty policy, bribery, and cheating. The email that was sent to the robotics judge was sent from your account. You must have something to say."

Jane gritted her teeth, trying to fight back the tears that threatened to come. She was not going to cry in front of these people.

"I don't have anything to say," said Jane.

"Then you leave us with no choice," said the man, looking at Jane regretfully. "I hate to do this…you're one of our most promising students. But, Malvern University has very high ethical standards. We can't let this type of behavior go unpunished. Your friends have already left Malvern of their own accord. As of today, we're also going to have ask you to leave the school.…"

"Wait just a moment," interrupted a deep voice.

Jane looked behind her in surprise. Her favorite teacher, Professor Chatham, was standing in the back of the room, holding a large envelope.

"I would like to enter an exhibit into the official inquiry file. He handed the envelope to the man who had been speaking. "This is a statement from John Westin…a confession of sorts. It explains everything that happened. If you read it, I think you'll change your mind regarding Jane."

The man took the letter, carefully read the contents, and thought for a moment.

"Jane, could you and Professor Chatham please leave the room for a few minutes?" he said. "We'll let you know when we reach a decision."

Professor Chatham took Jane gently by the arm and led her out of the room. There was a bench in the hallway and the two sat down.

"You were going to let yourself get expelled, weren't you?" asked Professor Chatham, gently.

The tears that Jane had been fighting against all morning began to spill down her face. She shrugged her shoulders and didn't say anything.

"I know you've been through a lot over the past week," he said, patting her hand. "But that doesn't give you an excuse to give up."

"But everything's over," she said. "You heard them. I'm being kicked out. After everything that happened I'm not sure I even want to do computer work anymore."

Professor Chatham shook his head in disagreement. "You were born to be a computer scientist. You're brilliant! I'm not about to let your talents go to waste. Plus, you won't be expelled. That letter from John exonerates you from all blame. You'll probably get suspended for a few days at the most."

Jane tried to look pleased, but failed. "I don't think I care anymore," she said.

"You have to care," said Professor Chatham, his voice betraying his excitement. "You have to continue your research. I wasn't going to tell you this until later, but that rabbit, the last one that got scanned, it's still alive. Your scanner did something to it. Its brain has nearly healed itself!"

Jane looked at Professor Chatham in amazement. "What? How is that possible?"

"I'm not sure," answered Professor Chatham. "But I need you to fix your scanner and then study that rabbit. I think you're onto something incredible!"

Jane's manner, which had been forlorn and dejected, suddenly changed completely. If her research could save lives, then she had to pursue it.

Just then, one of the members of the board opened the door softly and stepped up to Jane and Professor Chatham. "Jane," she said gently. "We're ready with our decision…."

***

"Is everything okay in here?" asked a friendly voice.

Jane started. She hadn't realized anyone else was in the office.

"Of course," mumbled Jane unconvincingly, as she attempted to drag herself back to the present.

"What are you doing here so late?" she asked the elderly man who was poking his head around her door.

"Oh you know how it is," said the professor. "There's always work to do."

"Do you mind if I come in?" he asked.

"Of course not," said Jane. "Please do."

Jane smiled as Professor Chatham made his way slowly into her office. He was the head of the computer science department at Malvern University. The two had met during Jane's first week at school. He had been her mentor while she was a student and was now a valued friend and colleague.

Professor Chatham settled into one of the chairs in Jane's office and said, "I'm actually trying to finish up some grant applications for the department. Hopefully it will appease the dean, for a little while at least."

Jane nodded understandingly. "I know you're under a lot of pressure right now. How do our chances look for the grants?"

"Not great," said Professor Chatham. "But something will come through for us…"

"I wish there was something I could do to help," said Jane.

"You're already helping," he replied. "Anyway, you work much too hard as it is. And, now that I look at you more closely, you look very tired and stressed. You aren't overdoing it again, are you? You know what I told you about that."

"I am stressed, but it's not because of work," Jane said, hesitantly. "It's because I just talked to Remy Crofton."

Jane hadn't planned on telling Professor Chatham about Remy, but, as he sat there before her, she couldn't help herself. He would probably figure it out anyway. He always knew when something was wrong.

Professor Chatham sat up. "Oh," he said, his brow creased in concern. "Are you okay?"

"Yes… no… I don't know," said Jane. "It's the first time I've talked to him in five years."

"I was thinking about that," said the professor, slowly. "That's actually why I stopped in to check on you. Today's the anniversary of when it all happened, right?"

Jane nodded her head numbly.

Professor Chatham shook his head sadly, "I had such high hopes for Remy and John. They were so intelligent. But I suppose that isn't enough."

"No," said Jane, "not in their case."

"What did he want?" asked Professor Chatham.

"You know him too well," said Jane, with a sharp laugh. "Of course he wanted something. He'd never call me for any other reason."

Jane took a deep breath. "Sorry," she said. "As you can see, I'm still upset. He wants to meet with me. He and John are in town to launch a new product. I think

16

they want my help with something, but Remy wasn't very specific."

"So what are you going to do?" asked Professor Chatham.

Jane look at him, shocked. "What am I going to do?!" she repeated. "You don't think I'd consider seeing either of them, do you?!"

Professor Chatham shrugged. "Aren't you at all curious? I was just reading an article about their company the other day. They've been incredibly successful."

"I'm not in the least bit curious!" said Jane, emphatically. "Anything that Remy's involved in isn't going to be good. We both know that."

Professor Chatham smiled slightly, "If only the dean could hear you now! Passing up a chance to meet with two millionaires who've offered to donate money to the department!"

Jane scoffed. "I don't care what the dean thinks. Plus, you know that if the department accepted any money from RJ Robotics there would be strings attached. The last offer they made was ridiculous! The computer science department isn't here to do research for Remy."

"Oh, I know," said Professor Chatham. "We both feel the same way about research funding. The whole purpose of this department is to conduct research that improves people's lives. It shouldn't be about making money, as the dean seems to think."

"Anyway, I wasn't suggesting that you work with Remy," Professor Chatham continued. "But you should at least find out what he wants."

Jane shook her head. "After all that Remy did to your poor nephew I don't know how you can even mention his name without getting angry!"

"I know," sighed Professor Chatham. "Remy was a

very bad influence, but Will would have gotten into trouble no matter who was around. He had a lot of lessons to learn, but I think he's finally learned them. He's really started to turn his life around."

"You didn't tell me that!" said Jane, eager to change the subject from Remy.

Professor Chatham smiled. "It's all happened gradually. But it's wonderful! He's going back to school, he's started working with his voice teacher again, and he's doing volunteer work. It's like he's a new person."

"That's great!" Jane smiled backed at him. "But what do you mean voice teacher . . . Will can sing?"

"Oh yes," said Professor Chatham happily. "You should hear him. He has a voice like an angel."

Jane laughed. "I find that hard to believe!"

"Next time you see him, ask him to sing something for you," replied Professor Chatham. "I'm sure he'd love to hear from you."

Jane blushed. "Maybe I'll drop by the bar one of these days. I haven't seen Will in such a long time."

"I know he'd like that," said Professor Chatham. "But that doesn't solve the real problem. What are you going to do about Remy?"

"I don't know. I told him never to contact me again just a few minutes ago. Maybe that took care of it," said Jane.

"Remy isn't going to give up that easily," he said.

Jane sighed in resignation. "I know..."

"Jane, you've been buried in this lab for the past five years," said Professor Chatham, gently. "Avoiding Remy, avoiding the world, avoiding anything that might hurt you. Isn't it time you ventured outside?"

"No!" replied Jane, vehemently. "I'm perfectly happy here."

"You can't spend the rest of your life in an outdated old lab with an outdated old man," said Professor

Chatham, with a small smile.

"You're not outdated!" protested Jane. "Plus, it's safe here. And Remy's not safe. Why should I see him again and jeopardize everything I've worked for?"

"Until you face your past and make peace with it, it's going to control your future," said Professor Chatham softly. "You need to live your life, not hide from it.

"I'm not hiding," said Jane, "at least not really...."

"Everyone dies, but not everyone lives," he said, musingly. "Don't you want to live?"

Jane sat for a moment in silence, and then she sighed in frustration. "Why are you always right?"

Professor Chatham smiled. "Every story needs a wise old man."

00000011

SOUP KITCHEN

"And a little extra for the two of you," said Will, as he slid two chocolate chip cookies onto a plate and handed it to a petite woman who was standing in line.

The woman beamed at Will and looked down at her two small children. "You're always so thoughtful, Will" she said.

"Anything for you, Mary," said Will, with a smile.

Mary put the plate of cookies on her tray, which was already loaded with food. She gave Will one last smile, and then went to find a place to sit in the crowded room, her children in tow.

Will waved at Mary's children and then turned to the next person in line.

"And what can I get for you today, Mr. Delancey?" he asked a tall, older man who was leaning heavily on a cane.

"Whatever you've got," sighed Mr. Delancey. "But nothing with…."

"Carrots," interrupted Will. "I know you hate carrots!"

A smile spread over Mr. Delancey's tired face. "You always remember."

Will laughed. "I don't like carrots that much either," he said, as he arranged some food on a plate.

"Here you go," he said. "Lots of chicken, mashed potatoes, and green beans, but no carrots."

"Thank you," said Mr. Delancey, "you're wonderful."

Will smiled and looked around the large soup

kitchen. He was a dedicated volunteer, coming several days a week. He enjoyed the work, but there was more to his volunteering. Will had grown up poor and under difficult circumstances.

"I don't know what I would have done without this place," said Will to himself, shaking his head. "This place and my uncle really saved me."

Will's smile broadened as he thought about his current situation. He'd drifted around for years, bartending, doing odd jobs, and trying hard to stay out of trouble. But now, things were finally coming together. He was back in school studying music. This time, he was determined to get his degree. He was even spending time at the local children's hospital doing his illusionist routine. He hadn't done magic tricks in years, but he hadn't lost the knack.

"Daydreaming again?" said a jocular voice at his shoulder.

Will started, lost in his own thoughts. "Jack!" he said, to a teenage boy who was standing at his shoulder . "I didn't know you were here today! You shouldn't sneak up on people like that!"

Jack was another volunteer at the soup kitchen. He reminded Will of his teenaged self....street smart, overly sure of himself, and always making the wrong decisions. Jack had been coming to the soup kitchen for the last few months, completing community service hours.

"Wanna help me wipe down some of the tables?" asked Jack, pointing towards some sponges and a bucket. "Mrs. Smith says she wants them super clean this time."

"Of course," said Will, grabbing one of the sponges. "We'll dazzle Mrs. Smith with our cleaning skills."

Jack laughed and took the other sponge and the bucket.

"Did I tell you about the last game?" asked Jack,

excitedly.

Will smiled. He'd encouraged Jack to get involved in sports at school as a way to keep out of trouble. And it had worked! Jack, despite being short and stocky, was an incredible basketball player. Will knew the school had won its last few games. He was sure Jack had played a starring role.

"No," said Will, "but I want to hear all about it."

Jack began talking animatedly. Will listened as closely as he could, but he was lost after a few moments. Basketball had never been his forte.

Suddenly, Jack paused in his story and grabbed Will's arm. "Who's that guy over there?" he whispered, pointing towards a man sitting by himself at one of the tables. "Mrs. Smith said there's some mystery about him, but she wouldn't tell me. She said you knew all about it."

Will looked towards where Jack was pointing. The man at the table was in his seventies, about medium height, and neatly dressed. He was clearly enjoying the food, digging into several large bowls and plates that were spread out before him. He was one of the regulars, but he was never very talkative. However, he always talked to Will.

"Wouldn't you like to know…" said Will, with a mysterious smile.

"Oh come on," said Jake, "you can't leave me hanging like that. I need to know! If you tell me, I'll clean all the pots and pans today! I swear!"

"Alright," said Will. "But you can't tell Mrs. Smith. I don't want her to think I'm slacking off."

"Of course," said Jack, eagerly. "Just tell me who he is."

"He's Matthew Armstrong," said Will quietly. "I'm sure you've heard of him."

"The crazy old millionaire who lives in the haunted

house?!" whispered Jake. "I thought he never came out!"

Jake tried hard not to stare at the man. "Wow! He does look crazy, just like everyone says!"

"He's not crazy," said Will, "but he is a little eccentric. He used to be a famous classical pianist. He travelled all over the world before he settled down here."

"How do you know all of this?" asked Jake.

"We're friends," smiled Will.

"You're friends with everyone, even the crazies!" said Jake. "But why does he come here? He's supposed to be rich!"

"He is," replied Will. "But he's been coming here for years. I have no idea why. Maybe he doesn't like to spend money."

"Or maybe it's the great food," laughed Jake. "Mrs. Smith does make a pretty mean meatloaf."

"And," added Will, "speaking of Mrs. Smith, I think we'd better get to work. She's giving us a very meaningful look."

Jake looked over to the kitchen where Mrs. Smith, the head cook and manager, was standing. She was staring at them fixedly and shaking her head.

"Alright," smiled Jake. "I'll make these tables shine! I don't want to get on Mrs. Smith's bad side. She promised me a chocolate cake next week for my birthday. I don't want her to change her mind. Last year she made me...."

Jake trailed off, his attention diverted by a newcomer who was standing in the doorway of the soup kitchen.

"Ugh," he said, wrinkling his face in disgust. "Your creepy friend Remy's here again! Why does he keep stopping by?"

"I have no idea," Will sighed. "I'll go see what he wants this time."

24

00000100

JOHN

A few days later, Jane was leaving work for the evening. It had been another long, discouraging day working on her research, which was going painfully slow. Jane used her VCS to secure the door to the lab, which locked with a loud click. "I'm getting nowhere fast," she sighed.

As Jane walked out of the building and towards the bus stop, she thought about what she was doing. Her research was so important, but it was going to take her years to finish. She knew her work wasn't glamourous and wouldn't make the college rich. But still, it could help so many people. Why couldn't anyone see that?

"It's always about money," grumbled Jane to herself, as she waited at the bus stop.

Jane, lost in her own thoughts, was suddenly startled by a loud noise. A flashy red sports car was speeding down the road towards her. Jane rolled her eyes.

"Rich kids," she mumbled to herself, in annoyance

The car screeched to a halt beside Jane. The passenger side window rolled down and a voice said, "Get in!"

Jane was taken aback. She didn't know anyone who owned such an expensive car. What was going on?

Jane peered into the window uncertainly. Suddenly, she froze in shock. She felt a bit shaky and put her hand on the car door to steady herself.

"John?" she whispered, her voice catching in her

throat.

John looked shaken as well. "Jane," he said softly. "It's good to see you. You look beautiful."

Jane smiled slightly. John hadn't changed.

"You don't look too bad yourself," she replied.

"Too much good living," laughed John, patting his stomach, which had filled out a little since Jane had seen him last. John, although completely unaware of it, was very good looking. He was the best looking computer nerd that Jane had ever met.

John pushed the passenger door open. "Why don't you get in? It'd be much nicer to catch up with you sitting next to me."

Jane was tempted to get in the car, but she stopped herself. "John," she said slowly, "why are you here?"

John looked away for a moment, his face reddening. He had never been good at hiding the truth.

"Remy sent you, didn't he?" she said, backing away from the car.

John nodded reluctantly. "Yes," he said, "but I would have come anyway. It's been way too long. It's time we were friends again. I've really missed you."

Jane looked at John, her heart softening in spite of herself. "I've missed you too," said Jane. "But I don't think I can go with you. We can't just pick things up again like nothing happened."

"I know," said John, seriously. "I want to make up for the past. But you need to give me a chance. Please, just spend a few hours with me...just the two of us. No one else."

Jane looked at John uncertainly. "You promise that it's just us? No Remy?"

"I promise," said John, "Remy will not be a part of our evening together. We don't even have to mention his name."

After another moment of hesitation, Jane slid into the

car. She wasn't sure if she was doing the right thing. But seeing John again had made her realize how much she missed his friendship.

"Let's drive somewhere," said Jane. "This is probably my only chance of being in one of these fancy cars. I should try to make the most of it."

John smiled. "How about we drive by the river and then we'll stop at the bar on the way back? We can see Mr. Lee and Will. It'll be like the old days again."

Jane returned John's smile. "Alright," she said. "But only if we can get something to eat while we're there. I haven't eaten all day."

"Of course!" said John. "We'll get our usual…my treat."

***

They were silent for a few moments while John drove along the river.

John touched the controls of the car, switching the car into self driving mode. Then, he cleared his throat awkwardly and said, "I hope you know how sorry I am for everything that happened. I don't know how things got so out of hand…"

"It's okay," said Jane softly. "When Remy gets involved, things never go as planned."

"But I let you down," said John, "I should have been there for you and I wasn't."

"I let that go long ago," said Jane. "Plus, you did help me. If it wasn't for your letter, I would have been kicked out of school."

John waved his hand dismissively. "It was much too little, much too late."

Jane looked out the window and sighed. Suddenly she felt very sad, as if she'd lost something special. She and John had been so close in college. For awhile she thought that he might be the one. But it wasn't to be.

"Let's not worry about the past right now," said Jane.

"I haven't seen you for so long. I want to enjoy our evening together."

John smiled and said, "That sounds like a great plan."

"So tell me," said Jane, "what have you been up to over the past five years?"

John laughed. "It's crazy when you say it like that," he said. "But I guess it really has been five years. I'm sure you know all about the company and how successful we've been. I never expected things to develop as they have. Remy and I were just two guys with some ideas."

"Two very smart guys with some pretty good ideas," interjected Jane.

"I guess," said John. "But I always thought you were the smartest. Much smarter than me or Remy. I figured you would be the one with all of the success."

"I chose a different path," said Jane.

John sighed. "I know," he said, his voice suddenly becoming grave. "Sometimes I wish I'd taken that path too. Your work regenerating neural pathways to heal damaged brains must be so fascinating and rewarding."

Jane looked at John in surprise. "How do you know so much about my work? I haven't even published that research yet."

John's face reddened and he replied, "Oh I know all about you, Jane. I hope it doesn't upset you that I've followed you over the years. Anyway, it turns out that people aren't really that hard to read. Mostly they do what you expect them to do. Some people choose a fate, like you. Most others simply travel the road they find themselves on. I guess that's what I've done. This life... it's not..." John broke off, unsure how to explain.

"I know," she said. "It's not exactly you."

John nodded. "I knew you'd understand. But I really can't complain. I've been able to do a lot of good. I've helped my family so much. They've never been so comfortable. All of my brothers and sisters can go to college now, and my parents were able to retire early. It's a good feeling to be there for them…they did so much for me."

Jane smiled at John. She knew how much he cared about his family. He had grown up without much money. His parents had both worked extremely hard, scrimping and saving, so John, their oldest, could go to college.

"I'm so glad," said Jane.

"And I guess I've done a few nice things for myself," said John, patting the steering wheel of the car.

"I don't even want to know how much this thing cost," said Jane. "I'd probably have a heart attack."

"Let's just say it was more expensive than the Fox," he smiled.

Jane laughed. John had driven an old broken down VW Fox during college. "That's probably a good thing!"

***

Lee's Bar, which had been John and Jane's hangout during college, was a hole in the wall place, down a little side street in town. Most of the college kids didn't know about it, and probably wouldn't have gone there if they did. It was a throwback to the past, and the passage of five years, with such huge advances in technology, now made it seem almost quaint. There were no robots, no VCS ordering, and Brain Bands were forbidden. Plastic coated menus, which had seen better days, listed the food and drink offerings. An actual human being took your order and normally, but completely delightfully, screwed something up. It was usually filled with regulars, working class people from town. But, what made the place special to John and Jane, was the food. The bar was owned by a Vietnamese man who cooked all of the food himself. It was some of the best food Jane had ever had.

"We'll have the usual," said John, as he sat down at one of the stools lined up in front of the grungy old bar.

Will looked up, startled. "Well!" he said in surprise. "It's been a long time since I've seen the two of you here!"

"Much too long," said Jane. "I bet you don't even remember our usual."

Will looked at Jane as if she were crazy. "How could I forget the usual?" he said, from behind the bar. "It would be like forgetting my own name. Plus, I never forget the order of a pretty girl."

"I think he's flirting with you," whispered John, as Will bustled behind the bar, getting them drinks.

"He's always flirting with me," said Jane, rolling her eyes. But then, suddenly, she looked at Will with more interest. She was thinking about what Professor Chatham had told her. Could Will really be making so many changes in his life?

Will turned around with two large glasses. "Water for the lovely Jane and the cheapest beer we have for John... unless you want to upgrade to something better. I saw your car out there."

"No," laughed John. "I'm good with the cheap stuff. I don't want to break with tradition."

"Will, your uncle told me that you're back in school," said Jane. "That's wonderful! He also told me that you sing like an angel," she added, with a smile. "Is that true?"

Will's face reddened and he squirmed uncomfortably. "Uh," he said, "I'd better go put your food order in. We can catch up later."

"I think you embarrassed him," said John, with a grin.

"I didn't think Will was the kind of person who got embarrassed," said Jane. "He always seemed so slick."

"People can change," said John, thoughtfully, "for

better or for worse."

Jane looked at John intently. "I feel like you're going to bring up Remy. Didn't we say he was off limits?"

"I actually wasn't thinking about Remy," replied John, "but if you don't want to talk about him we don't have to."

"No, it's okay," said Jane. "I don't mind. Being here with you makes everything seem easier, even Remy. But, if you tell me that Remy has changed for the better, I'm not going to believe you."

"No," laughed John. "Remy's never going to change. But he's different then he was in college. He's much more serious. He has big plans to change the world."

Jane looked skeptical. "I don't know," she said. "I don't think Remy's ever been serious about anything."

Just then, Will came back from the kitchen, bearing two large plates loaded with food.

"Here you go," he said, setting the plates down. "The vegetarian special…two 23's and two 36's, your usual. Mr. Lee started cooking as soon as he saw you walk in the bar. How's that for service?"

Jane smiled. "It's a good thing you both remembered, because I'm starving!"

00000101

ASHLEY

About an hour later, John and Jane were still sitting at the bar, chatting with Will and basking in the afterglow of a delicious meal.

"I need to come here more often," sighed Jane. "This food is so good."

"I wouldn't mind that," said Will. "You're a sight for sore eyes."

"Hey," said John. "What about me?"

"You're not that bad yourself," laughed Will, as he walked down the length of the bar to wait on another customer. "But never as good as Jane!"

"I suppose I should be getting home," sighed Jane, after Will had left. "I never stay out this late."

"Before we go," said John, "there's something I want to tell you."

He paused for a moment, as if gathering his courage. Then he began speaking quickly in a nervous voice. "I've been meaning to tell you this all evening. I don't know if you're going to understand, but it's important that you hear it from me first."

Jane looked at John curiously. "What is it?" she asked.

"You know when I said that people can change," he began. "I wasn't talking about Remy. I was actually talking about Ashley."

"Remy's sister?" Jane said, in surprise. "What does she have to do with anything?"

"She really has changed for the better," said John.

"We've been seeing a lot of each other over the past year or so, and, well..." John trailed off.

"Oh no," said Jane, looking at John in horror. "Please don't tell me that you and Ashley are...."

Just then, there was a loud commotion near the entrance to the bar.

"There you are, Johnny! I've been looking all over for you honey!" shouted Ashley, as she clomped into the bar, making sure everyone noticed her grand entrance.

John reddened and gave Jane one last imploring glance before he got up to meet Ashley.

Jane, left alone for a moment, groaned. Ashely of all people! What was John thinking? If only they had left the bar a few moments earlier. She would have been able to escape the coming ordeal.

"What are you doing in this dump?" asked Ashley, as John led her over to where Jane was sitting.

"Oh," said Ashley, as she caught sight of Jane. "That explains it. You always liked hanging out at lousy places."

"Hi Ashley," said Jane, dryly.

Ashley looked Jane over dismissively, as if she didn't exist, and said, "Hey Plain Jane."

"Well, is she going to talk to Remy?" asked Ashley, looking at John demandingly.

"You know I can hear you," said Jane. "If you have something to say, you can say it to me."

"Ooooh!" said Ashley, looking at Jane with new interest. "The little school girl has gotten sassy over the years."

"Now Ashley," began John, reprovingly.

"Oh shush, Johnny," said Ashley. "I don't mean anything by it. It's just our way. We always talk to each other like this. It shows how much we care. Right, Jane?"

"Sure," said Jane, suddenly feeling very tired. "And

no, Ashley, I wasn't planning on talking to your brother."

"Ha," crowed Ashley. "I told you so!" she said to John triumphantly. "She's scared, just like I said."

At that, Jane sat up straighter. "Scared…of Remy?" she said, scornfully.

"Of course you are," laughed Ashley. "Otherwise you would talk to him. But you can't…because you're scared."

"I'm tired, Ashley, and that's all there is to it. I had a long day. And some of us have to go to work tomorrow," said Jane.

"Tired can be fixed with a cup of coffee and a slap on the ass! To me it sounds like fear. But sure, head back to your safe little lab. Risk nothing, gain nothing…the story of your life," taunted Ashley.

Jane cringed at Ashley's words. She hated to admit it, but Ashley was partially right. She wasn't afraid of Remy, but she was afraid of disrupting her own life.

Jane knew that anything she said now would sound like a feeble excuse, but she tried one last time, "I am NOT afraid of Remy."

"Then you should be able to have a conversation with him," said Ashley, sweetly. "Right?"

"Fine," said Jane, sharply. "I'll talk to him right now if that's what you want!"

Ashley laughed gleefully and said, "This is going to be a night to remember!"

"Does anyone need anything?" interrupted Will, who had walked over to their end of the bar during Jane and Ashley's conversation.

"Will!" squealed Ashley, in delight. "I haven't seen you in ages! You look incredible!"

Will tried unsuccessfully to suppress a scowl. He had never been a fan of Ashley.

Ashley dangled her hand in front of Will, moving it back and forth so that the enormous diamond on her finger caught the light.

"I see you've acquired some new jewelry," he said, shortly.

"You noticed!" said Ashley, feigning surprise. "I guess it's hard not to notice," she continued. "It's the largest diamond that money can buy! Anyway, you missed your chance, Will. Me and Johnny are engaged!"

Will shrugged his shoulders. "Too bad," he said, sarcastically.

"Guess what we're doing tonight, Will?" asked Ashley, excitedly, undeterred by Will's manner. "We're all going to see Remy and he and Jane are going to have a cozy little chat. You're welcome to join us."

"Tempting," said Will, "but I have to work."

"Maybe some other time," said Ashely, smiling at him suggestively.

"Johnny, why don't you get the car for us," said Ashley. "I'll walk to the door with you. There are some people I think I know up front. We can tell them about our engagement and see if anyone else notices my ring."

"Sure, dear," answered John, who seemed oblivious to Ashley's behavior.

Ashley took John by the arm and the two walked towards the front of the bar.

"Jane," said Will, softly, "you don't have to go. You can stay here. I'll drive you home as soon as I get off work."

"Thanks," sighed Jane. "I appreciate the offer. But I have to go. If I don't face Remy now, I don't know if I ever will."

Will nodded, "I understand," he said. "But if you need anything, call me...I'll be there for you." Will scribbled his number on a piece of paper and pushed it towards her.

Jane took it, nodded her thanks at him, and headed into the unknown.

00000110

THE "CLUB"

John and Jane were silent as they drove to meet Remy. Ashley, sitting in the front seat next to John, chattered on and on, not seeming to mind that no one was listening to her.

Jane sighed and looked out the window. She wasn't sure if she was ready for this meeting. It had been good to see John again. In fact, she had really enjoyed her evening with him. But Remy was completely different. She wasn't scared of him. But she was scared of what he could do. There was something about Remy that seduced people. He was charming and charismatic, and something more that Jane couldn't quite describe. He had a way of making people do whatever he wanted, without them even being aware of it.

Jane had fallen under his spell once and she knew that Will had, all to horrible results. And it was clear that John was completely under his thumb.

"I can't let him get to me…not this time," she said to herself, resolutely.

After about twenty minutes of driving, John pulled into the parking lot of a seedy looking club on the outskirts of town.

Jane looked up at the flashing neon sign on the front of the building. "This isn't a strip club, is it?" she asked in disbelief.

John looked embarrassed. "Sorry," he began, "it's where Remy wanted to meet…"

"This isn't just any strip club," interrupted Ashley, with evident pride. "It's my strip club."

Jane looked at Ashley in surprise. "You own this place?"

"Yes I do! So you better behave yourself while you're here. Because if you cause any trouble, you'll be at the pole... dancing!"

Ashley laughed, reveling in her own joke. Jane had no response. She could only shake her head, sadly. Poor John. This was the woman he was going to marry.

The three entered the club, with Ashley leading the way. Jane could sense a change in the atmosphere as soon as they walked through the front entrance. The music was still blaringly loud, but it felt as if a hush had fallen over the entire place. It was clear that the women who worked at the club were scared of Ashley. Everyone seemed anxious to avoid her notice.

As Jane surveyed the room, information and statistics began to appear in her VCS. Superimposed over each of the "employees" at the club were prices, measurements, statistics, and preferences that caused Jane to blush.

"Remy's in the back room," said Ashley, as she looked around her domain with pleasure. "It's a special part of the club, just for him. I'll bring you back there. It's a little tricky to find."

Ashley took the lead again, scolding and upbraiding her "employees" as they made their way to the back of the club. At the end of a dark hallway, Ashley turned sharply to the right and then pushed open a large, heavy door.

"You've got visitors!" she announced, as they walked into the room.

Jane took it all in with one glance. Remy was sitting on a plush sofa with three strippers, each vying for his attention. This room was very different from where they had just come from. It was clean, bright and blindingly white. As she crossed the threshold of the "back room" all of the vital statistics that had been scrolling through her VCS just a moment ago suddenly vanished. Her VCS was no longer functioning.

"Ashley," said Remy in annoyance, "you know I hate to be interrupted when I'm entertaining…." his voice trailed off as he saw John and Jane standing behind Ashley.

"I'm sorry ladies," said Remy, with his dazzling smile. "I think I'm going to have to take a raincheck. We'll have to do this some other time."

The girls pouted and whined, genuinely disappointed that they had to leave.

"Remy's even got them charmed," thought Jane to herself, as the girls gathered their few items of clothing and left the room.

"You better get to work as soon as you get back out there," shouted Ashley. "No slacking off!"

"It's so hard to find good workers these days," she grinned, as she plopped down next to Remy on the sofa.

"Did you miss me, big brother?" cooed Ashley, as she cuddled up next to him.

Jane looked at them in uncomfortable fascination. They had such a strange relationship for a brother and sister. It had never made any sense to her. They were either screaming at each other or flirting like hormonal high school students.

"Of course," said Remy, patting her on the head. "And I missed these two almost as much," he smiled, gesturing towards Jane and John, who were still standing.

Remy got up from the couch clumsily. He made an attempt to set his champagne glass on the table in front of him, but instead it dropped from his hand and spilled everywhere.

"Hello, John," he said, stumbling awkwardly towards the two. "Why don't you sit over there?"

"And Jane," he slurred drunkenly, pausing in front of her. "Thanks for coming. I didn't think you would."

Jane nodded coldly, steeling herself for what might happen next. Remy after a night of drinking was never a good thing.

"Why don't you sit down over there and then we can have a nice, long chat," he said.

"By the way, your Brain Bands won't work in here," he continued, "only mine does. It's a little security feature I set up. You know how it is...you can never be too careful!"

"Can I get you anything...something to drink or eat?" asked Remy. "For a strip club, this place has really great food. But that's no surprise with Ashley running things. Only the best for my little sister."

Ashley giggled and smiled at her brother as he sat down again next to her.

"We're fine," said Jane, shortly. "Why don't you tell me what you want?" she said, looking directly at Remy. "I don't have much time."

"Always so serious," said Remy, amiably. "You haven't changed Jane. But you're right, it's getting late and I don't want to keep you out all night."

"Did you and John talk about my offer this evening?" he asked.

Jane shook her head. "No, "she said, "we only talked about nice things."

"I thought it would be better coming from you," interrupted John. "You're much better at explaining this kind of stuff."

"That's true," laughed Remy. "John here isn't much of a salesperson."

"It's actually very simple," he continued. "RJ Robotics is at a turning point. We're about to start

40

developing a new product line, but we need your expertise to get things going. If we're successful, we'll be trillionaires!"

"I don't understand," said Jane in surprise. "My expertise, as you call it, has nothing to do with building service robots or Brain Bands! And my work certainly won't make you any money!"

Remy waved his hand dismissively. "Jane, Jane, Jane," he said airily. "When are you going to get it into your head that I'm not the evil person that you think I am? I'm not just about making money. Sheesh! Fry a few bunny brains, and you'd think I was the devil himself!" he laughed.

Ashley looked over at Remy and began laughing uncontrollably, as if "fried bunny brains" was the most hilarious thing she had ever heard.

Jane looked at the two laughing and she felt her eyes sting with tears. How could she be in the same room with these people? They hadn't changed. They were just as horrible now as they were five years ago in the lab at Malvern. The entire evening had been a huge mistake.

"John," said Jane desperately. "Please get me out of here now."

John nodded dumbly as he took Jane by the hand and led her out of the room, leaving Remy and Ashley still laughing.

00000111

SECOND OFFER

A few days later, Jane was sitting at her favorite coffee shop. It was a Saturday, and she was looking forward to a peaceful afternoon. She needed a break after all of the stress she'd been under. The last few days had been difficult, but Jane was proud that she'd made it through. She had spoken to John again and finally confronted Remy. She felt as if a chapter of her life had closed.

Jane looked out the large window and smiled. Late summer was her favorite time of year. The trees on the street were a beautiful shade of green and the weather was pleasantly warm. Maybe she would take a walk along the river after her coffee. It was the perfect day for it.

Jane turned her eyes from the street outside to the book that was propped open in front of her. She read a few sentences, and then her mind began to wander. She looked around the coffee shop absently as she sipped her coffee.

The coffee shop, although crowded with people, was eerily quiet. Brain Bands, ubiquitous everywhere, had changed the way people socialized. Jane had thought cell phones were bad, but Brain Bands were worse. People were sitting in small groups, but they weren't looking at each other or talking to each other. Instead, they were gazing into the distance, their gazes slightly unfocused...a tell tale sign of Brain Band usage. People were addicted…constantly using their Brain Bands to surf the internet, update social media, watch viral videos, and get bombarded with ads and commercials.

She was probably the only one in the entire coffee shop who wasn't using a Brain Band. Except for…

Suddenly Jane stiffened. Directly across the room from her, staring at her intently, was Remy.

Jane immediately began to gather up her things in order to leave. This was getting ridiculous. She had assumed they were finished after the incident at the club. Was Remy ever going to leave her alone?

Remy walked quickly over to Jane and sat on the stool next to her. "Aren't you going to let me explain?" asked Remy, giving her his most charming smile.

"I wasn't really myself the other night," he said, touching her arm and gently pushing her back down into her stool. "I'd been celebrating a little too much and might have been just a tad drunk."

"A tad?" said Jane, derisively.

"Well, maybe a bit more than a tad," said Remy. "But you know how I get when I'm drinking. I turn into a monster."

Remy did have a point. Jane had seen him in action several times during their college days together. He was a different person when he was drunk.

"I'm really sorry about the other night," he continued. "I didn't mean any of the horrible things that I said. I still want to talk to you. Listen to what I have to say, and then, if you don't want to talk to me ever again, I understand. After this, I'll leave you alone. I promise. Just give me a chance."

Jane looked at Remy and sighed. It seemed that she was never going to escape from him unless she let him have his say. Being drunk wasn't an excuse for his behavior, but she was willing to listen for a few minutes, especially if it meant that she would be free of him. Plus,

44

being on her own turf and not at Ashley's seedy club made her feel a little more comfortable talking to him.

"Alright," said Jane finally, as she looked at her watch. "You have ten minutes, and then I'm leaving."

"Thank you," he said, "you won't regret this."

Remy took a deep breath and began speaking quickly.

"Since its founding, RJ Robotics has focused mainly on service and industrial robots. We've done some amazing things in the past few years. But we're at a crossroads now. We want to take the next technological leap into humanoid robots. John and I are brilliant, but we don't have your expertise in biomimicry. John can handle the algorithm optimization and I can do the market prediction and trend analysis. But we need you to implement the hardware and run the simulations."

Jane looked at Remy skeptically. "That's it? That's all you want? Hardware simulations? There must be a catch."

Remy laughed. "There is no catch! I'll admit, I haven't always been honest in the past. But John's been a good influence on me. I'm not holding anything back. I swear!"

"Look," said Remy, persuasively, "if you come help us, you'll be a millionaire in no time! You'll get credit for all of the amazing work that you do for us. You'll be famous!"

Jane shook her head slowly. "You really don't get me, Remy," she said. "For me, it's not about any of those things. I don't care about being rich or famous. I'm following this career because I truly believe that I can do good and make the world a better place with my research."

Remy looked at Jane and laughed. "I don't believe you! No one is as good as you make yourself out to be. But how about this as a motivator….if you come help us, you can use our lab facilities for your own research.

Your work will advance by leaps and bounds. Instead of rotting in that crappy college lab for the next ten years, you'll be able to finish things in a few months. We have the resources. We're willing to give you anything you need, if you help us."

Jane was at a loss for words. This wasn't the approach she had expected Remy to take. His offer was tempting! But at what cost? Remy never provided anything without exacting a considerable price.

"I don't know...." said Jane slowly.

"That's better than no!" said Remy excitedly. "We're making progress."

"I didn't say anything definite," replied Jane firmly. "I just said I don't know."

"How about this," said Remy eagerly. "RJ Robotics is having a big party next Friday at my house on the island. We're launching a new robot and celebrating John and Ashley's engagement. Why don't you come? You can enjoy yourself at the party and then spend a few days checking out the research facility. No strings attached!"

Jane still didn't know what to say. "Why don't you give me a night to sleep on it?" she said. "I need some time to think."

Remy jumped up in excitement. "I know you won't regret it!" he almost shouted. "It'll be just like old times with you, me, and John working together! Remember our plan in college...it was RJJ Robotics, for all three of us. Maybe we should change the name!"

"I didn't say yes," protested Jane.

"I know," said Remy. "But I know you're going to. I can't wait to tell John! He's going to be so excited! The three Amigas, back together again!"

--

The next day, Jane stopped by the computer lab. She knew that she'd find Professor Chatham. She'd spent the night tossing and turning, and she was still no closer to a decision now than she'd been the night before. She was hoping he could give her some good advice.

"Why Jane," said the professor, in surprise, as she poked her head into his office. "I thought I told you to take the weekend off. You need a break!"

"What about you?" smiled Jane, as she sat down in one of the chairs in his office. "Don't you ever get a break?"

Professor Chatham sighed. "No rest for the weary," he said, with a frown. "I have the trustees breathing down my neck, as usual. If I don't figure out something soon, I don't think this department is going to last. At least not the way it has been."

Jane looked at Professor Chatham with sympathy. "You've been such an incredible leader of the department. I don't know why they aren't grateful to have you."

"You know as well as I do what the college wants," said Professor Chatham. "Our department isn't like the football team. We don't make money for the school. But they think that we should."

Jane nodded. "It's always about money," she said ruefully.

"But you didn't come here on a Sunday morning to listen to me complain," said Professor Chatham. "I can see that something's bothering you. What is it?"

"Am I that obvious?" laughed Jane.

"I know you too well," said Professor Chatham. "When you get that look on your face I know there's something wrong."

"It's Remy again," said Jane. "I talked to him yesterday."

"Oh," replied Professor Chatham. "I'm glad you survived."

47

"It wasn't quite as bad as I thought it would be," said Jane. "Remy wants me to come work in his lab, at least temporarily. He and John want my help developing a new line of humanoid robots. While I'm there, he said I could pursue my own research…speed things up by years!"

Professor Chatham nodded slowly. "I see," he said. "And what did you say?"

"I told him that I'd sleep on it and give him an answer today," replied Jane.

"Which is why you're here," said Professor Chatham. "To seek the advice of an old man!"

"To seek the advice of a wise man," said Jane. "You've never steered me in the wrong direction."

"Is that so?" smiled Professor Chatham. "I guess I'm wiser than I give myself credit for! But you've always come to the right decisions yourself. I just listen."

Jane smiled. "So you're saying I have to figure this one out for myself?"

"I'm fairly certain you've already figured it out," replied Professor Chatham.

"I assume you're going to need a little time off," he added.

Jane thought for a moment and then laughed. "I guess I do," she said, "but only a few days…a week at the most."

Professor Chatham smiled. "It's time for you to spread your wings and fly."

"I don't know," said Jane, uncertainly. "I'm still not sure this is the right thing to do."

"I know you're ready for this," said Professor Chatham, confidently. "But just remember to be careful out there. Don't fly too close to the sun."

"I'll be careful," said Jane, seriously. "I promise."

00001000

ARRIVAL

For at least the hundredth time that day, Jane wondered if she had made the right decision. Perhaps this entire thing was a huge mistake.

Jane was waiting at a small pier for the boat that would bring her to the Crofton family island. She had always known Remy was wealthy, but until now, she hadn't realized just how wealthy he was. The family owned several small islands in the bay, and on one of them they had built a sprawling mansion. The party was going to take place on the grounds of the mansion that evening. Jane didn't generally like parties, and she was dreading this one.

Jane looked down at her bags on the ground next to her and smiled. She had brought Bunnykins with her. The sight of the rabbit in the small carrier made her feel better.

"What do you think, Bunnykins?" she said, bending down to get closer. "Did I make the right decision?"

Bunnykins hopped around in her carrier, clearly anxious to be let out.

"Not too much longer," said Jane, reassuringly.

As she spoke, Jane heard the sound of an approaching boat. She looked up to see a sleek yacht heading towards the pier.

Jane laughed as she saw it. She didn't know why, but she'd been expecting a dumpy old tugboat. Of course, Remy would only have the very best.

As the vessel reached the pier, Jane was impressed at how effortlessly the pilot maneuvered the craft.

"Remy always used to say he wanted to automate the entire world," mused Jane. She assumed that the yacht was piloted by computer.

Jane watched the crew scurry about the boat. There were two men on board, busy making the ship fast to the pier.

Jane picked up Bunnykins' carrier carefully. She was about to grab her other bags, when one of the men on the boat leapt to the pier, walked over to her, and put out his hand.

Jane smiled and took his hand.

"Hi," she said, expecting him to shake her hand in greeting and introduce himself. Instead, he squeezed her hand for a moment and looked at her closely.

"Welcome....Jane," he said slowly.

Before Jane could say anything, the man had already turned away. "I'll get your bags," he said.

"I don't mind carrying them myself," began Jane. But her words were lost on the man. He had already picked up her bags and was heading towards the boat.

Jane walked up a short gangplank where she was met by another man, who also took her hand.

He shook her hand and said, "Welcome aboard, Jane. My name is Rob. We have a twenty minute ride out to the island. You can make yourself comfortable below deck. Everything you might want is there."

"Thanks, Rob," replied Jane, "it's nice to meet you."

Rob looked at her vaguely and then paused for a moment. Finally, he nodded and said, "It's nice to meet you too."

"Here," said Rob, holding out a Brain Band to Jane. "Mr. Crofton suggested that you wear this on the ride over."

Jane almost groaned. Not another Brain Band!

"That's okay," replied Jane. "I already have one."

"But this is a special Brain Band, just for you," replied Rob.

"Really," said Jane, "I'm fine with mine."

"Mr. Crofton was very insistent," said Rob. "He's going to be extremely disappointed."

"I'm sorry," said Jane firmly, "but he's going to have to be disappointed."

Rob shook his head, clearly disapproving Jane's decision. He took her arm and led her below, and then he left without saying another word. Jane shrugged her shoulders at his odd behavior. Being on the water all the time must do something to people.

Jane looked around the interior of the boat. It was just as luxurious as the exterior. And Rob was right, there was everything that she could ever want, including rabbit treats for Bunnykins.

Jane sank into a soft, overstuffed chair and smiled slightly. "I could get used to this," she said.

***

A few moments later, Jane felt a gentle hand on her shoulder. She slowly opened her eyes to see Rob standing over her.

"We've arrived," he said.

Jane sat up and looked around groggily. She must have fallen asleep during the trip.

Jane rubbed her eyes and stood up slowly. "Sorry," she said. "I never fall asleep like that. I don't know what's wrong with me. It must be all of this fresh sea air," she joked.

But her pleasantries were lost on Rob. He looked at her for a moment in confusion and then beckoned for her to follow him. Jane grabbed Bunnykins' carrier and hurried after Rob. Once on deck, Jane could see the shadowy outline of the island before her, looming out of the early evening darkness.

She shivered, even though it wasn't cold out. There was something so isolated and forlorn about the place. She felt very alone. Jane looked down at Bunnykins, who was sleeping peacefully in her carrier. She was thankful yet again that she had brought Bunnykins with her. At the very least she'd have one friendly face to look at.

As Jane descended the gangplank onto the island, she saw Remy running towards the boat.

"You're here!" he said excitedly. "I wasn't sure this was ever going to happen. But now it's real!"

Jane grimaced and walked towards Remy slowly. She still wasn't sure it should be happening, but it was too late now.

Remy was almost jumping up and down in his excitement. He grabbed her arm and began talking quickly.

"How did you like the yacht? I programmed that Brain Band especially for you! Did you notice the computer controlled stabilizer and the enhancements that showed the featured food and drink of the day? I also included statistics on the yacht itself and the names of the crew. What did you think?"

Jane felt a small twinge of guilt. So that was why Rob had been so adamant about the Brain Band! Remy wanted to impress her. Jane toyed with the idea of lying to Remy, but then she thought better of it. She was very bad at lying and Remy was a master. He would see right through her.

"Actually," confessed Jane, "I fell asleep on the way over."

Remy tried not to let the disappointment show on his face. "Oh well," he said. "I'm sure you'll have another opportunity while you're here. We can take the yacht out whenever you want."

"In the meantime," he continued. "We have lots to

do! I can't wait to give you a tour of the house. It's been in the family for years and goes back to the early 1900s. I know you love old stuff, so this will be perfect. And then you'll have just enough time to get ready for the party! It's going to be wild! People should start arriving in about an hour or so. I chartered four more boats to bring people over. Everyone is going to be here!"

Jane looked at Remy and tried to smile. It was going to be a long evening. "Shouldn't I get my bags?" she asked, as Remy led her towards the house.

"Don't worry about that," said Remy lightly. "Rob will see to your things."

"You're living in luxury now," he continued, with an imperious wave of his hand. "You don't have to do anything while you're here!"

***

As Jane and Remy entered the house, Ashley, who was all smiles, appeared in the doorway to greet them.

Jane couldn't remember Ashley ever being happy to see her.

"You're finally here!" she said, eagerly. "Remy said I could give you a tour of the house! I just had it redecorated last year. I did most of the design work myself, of course. I actually had to fire a few decorators. They just couldn't understand my vision…."

Jane half smiled to herself. Ashley wasn't excited to see her. She was excited to show off her exquisite taste in home furnishing. As Ashley babbled on, Jane looked around surreptitiously. She could certainly see the hand of Ashley in the décor. The nearest piece of furniture, an overstuffed bench, was upholstered with neon pink leopard print fabric.

"Aahh!" you noticed the bench," said Ashley, following Jane's gaze. "Isn't it incredible? It's an antique, but it was covered in the most hideous fabric I've ever seen. I had to special order this fabric, but it was worth it! Don't you just love it?"

"It's certainly unique," said Jane.

"I knew you'd love it," said Ashley, taking Jane's arm and leading her towards a large central stairwell. "That's why I gave you the leopard bedroom. There are fifteen guest rooms and they all have en suite bathrooms and a decorating theme. That was my idea! Remy thought you might want something quieter, but I know you'll love the leopard room. Everything is covered in leopard print fabric. It's beautiful!"

Jane tried to keep her face from showing her emotions. Part of her wanted to laugh and part of her wanted to cry. She couldn't imagine spending a week in a leopard print bedroom.

As the two walked up the stairs, with Remy following closely behind, Ashley continued talking. "Your timing is perfect! My engagement party is tonight and my birthday party is next Friday, the day before you're leaving. You're lucky that Remy wanted you here. I never would have invited you, but you're going to have the best time of your life! My parties are legendary. My birthday party is a 1920's themed costume party. Isn't that awesome?"

"Uh, Ashley," interrupted Remy, "do you think you could show Jane her bedroom later? I want to show her the museum."

"You're no fun!" moaned Ashley. "I've been waiting all day to show Jane around the house."

"It won't take me that long," replied Remy. "But I want her to see all of the progress that RJ Robotics has made. You can have her after that, at least until the party."

"Fine," said Ashley, "but don't keep me waiting too long. You don't want me to get impatient!"

"Don't worry," said Remy. "Just a few minutes."

Ashley stomped down the hallway, turning down the corridor that led towards the bedrooms.

"Sorry," said Remy. "You know how much she likes to talk. She hasn't had anyone except me to talk to all day. Plus, she's really proud of the house. She put a lot of effort into it."

"I can tell," said Jane, as she gazed at the leather wallpaper that lined the hallway. "It's very Ashley."

"She really does have a gift for decorating," said Remy, seriously.

Jane tried not to laugh and then, to change the subject, asked Remy, "What's the museum?"

"Just a small project I've been working on for the past few years," said Remy excitedly. "I've arranged all of the robots that RJ Robotics has ever built from the first prototype five years ago, to the model we're unveiling tonight. You can see the progression of the company and the technology. I think you'll find it fascinating!"

Jane nodded her head. She didn't usually agree with Remy, but she was actually excited to see the robots that he and John had built. She hadn't followed RJ Robotics too closely over the years, but she knew that they were responsible for many innovations in the field.

"Here we are!" said Remy, as he turned down a long, narrow hallway.

The hallway was lined on each side with glass cases.

The cases on the left wall housed robots with historical significance. It was clear that Remy had assembled a collection that showed the progression of robotic technology from its very beginnings to the present day.

Jane recognized the first robot immediately. It was a huge box on wheels, with a long radio antenna sticking out of the top. It looked like something straight out of a 1950's B-movie.

"Shakey!" said Jane, in astonishment. "Is this the

real one or a replica?" she asked.

"Of course it's the real one....on indefinite loan from the Computer History Museum in California," replied Remy.

"In our world, these old robots are priceless! How did you end up with so many of them?" asked Jane.

"RJ Robotics can exert an unimaginable influence when necessary," said Remy, with a smug smile.

Jane nodded and was silent. Perhaps it was better not to ask questions about the provenance of Remy's collection. She had the eerie feeling that she might unwittingly become an accessory after the fact if she learned too much.

Jane continued walking down the left wall, admiring the first fumbling attempts at Artificial Intelligence and machine automation. It was inspiring to see how much the field had advanced in just a few decades.

Creations from earlier in the century such as ASIMO, Baxter, and Roomba, shared space with early prototypes from Boston Dynamics, whose first awkward attempts at human and animal biomimicry, made Jane smile. She spent several moments marveling at OpenWorm, a simulation of all 302 neurons of the C. elegans nematode, which had inspired her own research.

When Jane reached the end of the left wall, she turned and began examining the glass cases that lined the right wall. This section of the "museum" highlighted the history of RJ Robotics. The first case held the prototype "Brain Band" and Jane almost laughed when she realized that it looked very similar to the VCS she had made for herself.

After that, there were several cases that displayed RJ Robotics first forays into "body hacking," including an exoskeleton designed to take motor signals from a human spinal chord and increase the strength of the wearer tenfold.

"Recognize this?" asked Remy, who had come up behind her.

Jane nodded. The exoskeleton was based on research that she, John, and Remy had started in college.

"You took our initial research in biocontrol algorithms and just ran with it," she said.

"Of course I did!" said Remy. "Why wait around for someone else to beat me to the punch? I saw a need in the market place and I filled it. It's as simple as that."

"But we had so little understanding back then," said Jane, thoughtfully. "Really, if you think about it, not that much has changed. There's so much that we still don't understand, even today."

"What does it matter?" asked Remy. "If the technology works, sell it. We can figure out all of the details later."

Jane shook her head in disagreement. "You sound like the students who've been virtual touring Malvern. They say the same thing. One of them even mentioned the control algorithm! I haven't thought about that since college. Can you believe we were naïve enough to think that we could discover an algorithm that unlocks all of the brain's subroutines?"

"Maybe we weren't so naïve," replied Remy. "I think there's still hope of finding it, and filling even more needs in the market place."

Jane shook her head. "You can't find something that doesn't exist," she said. "Plus, aren't there things that are more important than just filling a need in the market place? It can't be just about the money for you, can it?"

"Money. . . and power," said Remy, solemnly.

There was an awkward silence for a moment. Jane wanted to say more, but she knew it would fall on deaf ears. She and Remy saw the world so differently.

Jane sighed and turned her attention to the next case in the display, which held RJ1. RJ1 was RJ Robotics first commercially viable robot. It was little more than a scaled down version of BAXTER, with the addition of John's elegant AI programming, but it had been hugely successful. It was the first service robot that could fit in an average sized home and provide useful services.

"We sold over 3 million units in the first year!" Remy boasted. "That helped us to fund further R&D, and to create our next robot, the RJ2." Remy gestured towards the next case, which held a smaller, more streamlined version of the RJ1.

"Just look at the RJ2!" said Remy, admiringly, "quite an improvement over the first model! We were able to make it stronger, more mobile, more capable, and much more affordable!"

"You don't need to sell me on RJ Robotics," Jane replied. "I'm already impressed."

"What can I say? I'm passionate about my work!" laughed Remy.

Jane looked thoughtfully at the next few cases, which held examples of more recent robots, each one just a bit smaller and more efficiently designed than the last.

"I'm sure it's been a challenge to keep scaling everything down from the earlier models," she said.

"All in a day's work," said Remy, with a shrug, as if designing robots was the simplest task in the world.

"Look at this one!" said Remy, excitedly, as they reached the end of the row of glass cases. "It's our latest service robot. We're launching this model at the party tonight. This is serial number 1 of the 3 series. Their AI is much more advanced than any of our previous creations. They're in constant communication with each other through our mainframe. You'll have a chance to interact with them at the party. I think you'll be wowed!"

"I'm sure I will be," said Jane, as she looked at the museum, trying to take it all in.

"It's really amazing!" she said.

"I like having everything together like this," said Remy. "You can really see all of the progress we've made."

Jane nodded in agreement, and then asked, curiously. "What's this pedestal for? It's empty."

Jane gestured towards a tall pedestal that was placed in the center of the corridor. It looked as if it was being reserved for some special creation.

"That is the place of honor!" said Remy. "It's reserved for our greatest invention yet...the humanoid robot that I told you about. RJ Robotics is going to build the best humanoid robot in the history of robotics!"

"That's been the quest of roboticists for years," said Jane. "It's become something of a race. Who's going to build the best humanoid robot first?"

"There's no doubt about that.....especially if you're helping us!" said Remy. "RJ Robotics is always first!"

00001001

PARTY

Jane was standing on the edge of a large group of people, trying not to look as uncomfortable as she felt. The party was even worse than she had imagined. There were at least 200 people in attendance, all wealthy or famous. Everyone was dressed in expensive cocktail attire or designer evening wear. Remy had hired a DJ for the event and he was blasting loud rock music out over the crowd, some of whom were dancing. The noise was deafening. Most of the partygoers were gathered around Remy's pool, which was surrounded by a patio area with chairs and lounges.

There were a large number of service robots circulating gracefully about the pool area. The majority of the robots were of the new RJ3 series that Jane had seen in the museum. The main purpose of the party was to launch the robots, and it was clear that Remy was taking advantage of the opportunity to show off their advanced skills. The RJ3 series robots could actively balance on two wheels but had humanoid upper appendages. Their elegant design allowed them to navigate effortlessly amongst the crowd, serving food from small trays, collecting detritus, and interacting socially with the guests.

The other service robots at the party were of the less mobile RJ1 series robots. They were put to good use as bartenders, a task at which they were highly skilled. Due to the robots, the hors d'oeuvres and social lubricants were flowing with all of the speed and mechanical efficiency of a modern mainframe. It was an impressive, but slightly disturbing, sight.

Jane didn't know how she was going to make it through the next several hours. If she was more familiar with the mansion, she would have attempted to head back to her room. But the house was one vast maze to her. She knew she'd be lost in a few moments. She was just going to have to suffer through the party.

She had seen John for one brief moment at the beginning of the party. He'd started to talk with her, but Ashley had quickly interrupted and dragged him off to talk to someone more important. Remy was only a few feet away from her, but she had no intention of talking to him. He was drinking one cocktail after another and was surrounded by scantily clad women.

"At least Remy's having a good time," she thought to herself with a slight smile.

Jane looked around the crowded pool area again, trying to figure out what to do with herself. Maybe she could sit down? That would be nice, but it seemed as if every seat was taken. She was also starving, but too nervous to approach any of the service robots for food. She had hoped that one of them might approach her, but it seemed as if they weren't aware of her existence.

Then, almost as if reading her mind, a service robot glided noiselessly up to her.

"Good evening, Jane," said the robot.

"Hi," said Jane, a bit awkwardly. Despite being in the robotics field, social robots had never been her specialty. She wasn't sure exactly how to talk with one.

"I would offer you an hors d'oeuvres," said the robot, who was holding a tray filled with appetizers, "but these are not suitable for vegetarians."

Jane smiled. There was something oddly appealing about this robot. "How did you know I'm a vegetarian?"

62

asked Jane.

"As Service Model RJ3 Serial number 839, I am programmed to know the preferences of those I serve," answered the robot.

"Oh," said Jane. "I guess that makes sense. What else do you know?"

"I am programmed to provide entertainment. I know approximately 5000 jokes. Would you like to hear one?"

"No," said Jane, with a smile. "I don't need a joke. But do you mind if I ask you a question?"

"Do you mean a question in addition to the one you just asked?" said the robot.

Jane chuckled, mildly impressed, "Yes, exactly."

"Ask me anything. I am programmed to be of service."

"I have three oranges in a yellow box. I have a friend named Tom who has three red apples in a blue box . . ." began Jane.

The robot interrupted her, "Jane, because I am aware that you are a well known computer scientist, I am prepared to answer many Turing Test questions. However, is it not true that answering your question would serve little purpose? For you are already aware that I am a robot, Service Model RJ3 Serial number 839."

"That's a very good response Number 839," smiled Jane. "I'm impressed."

"I am glad to be of service and gratified to know that you find my programming satisfactory. Is there anything else I can provide for you?"

"I wish you could tell me how I'm going to get through this party," she sighed. "I think it's going to be a long night."

"You can interact with others," replied the robot. "That is what people do at parties. You are acquainted with Remy, John, and Ashley. They are your friends. I could introduce you to other guests. Then, they will be your friends too."

Jane laughed. "Thanks for the offer," she said. "But I think I'd rather just stay here."

"I must depart," said the robot. "I am needed at the bar to provide drinks for the guests. It was a pleasure speaking with you Jane."

"It was nice talking with you too, 839," said Jane, as she watched the robot glide back towards the bar.

Jane really was impressed. The robot had been able to converse with her in a very natural way, and was kind and polite. John must have been responsible for the programming. Remy would never have been able to pull off such a convincing version of care and concern.

"It's probably the only nice conversation I'll have this evening," said Jane ruefully, as she glanced at the chaotic partygoers around her. "The robots are more civilized than the guests!"

Suddenly, Jane felt a hand on her arm. She turned abruptly, ready to pull away from whoever was bothering her. She'd already been harassed by several drunk playboy types. She was hoping this wasn't going to be the pattern for the evening.

However, before she could say anything, a familiar voice said, "Now you're a sight for sore eyes!"

"Will!" said Jane, in delight. She had never been happier to see anyone in her life. She had always been a bit wary around Will, but right now, a friendly face was a godsend.

"I didn't know you were going to be here!" she said.

"I didn't know you were going to be here either!" smiled Will. "But now that we're both here, I'm glad I came. I was regretting coming as soon as I stepped off the boat. This isn't exactly my type of party."

Jane smiled in agreement, "I know," she said, looking around at the drunken crowd.

"Remy invited me, and I felt bad saying no," explained Will. "He keeps showing up at the soup kitchen where I volunteer."

"Remy working at a soup kitchen!" she said, in surprise. "That doesn't sound like the Remy I know."

Will laughed. "I didn't say he was helping out at the soup kitchen. He just shows up, looks around and then leaves. I asked him to help a few times but he looked at me like I was crazy."

"That's more like it," said Jane.

"I'm trying to give him the benefit of the doubt. Maybe he really does have a heart in there somewhere," said Will.

Jane looked over at Remy, who was now doing Jell-O shots with the girls. "I find that hard to believe," she said, gesturing in his direction. "He probably wants something from you."

Will looked where Jane was pointing. "Oh my," he said. "You have a point. Remy never does anything that doesn't benefit number one!"

"By the way," said Will, looking back towards Jane. "You look lovely this evening."

Jane looked down at herself in surprise. She had been feeling very plain and underdressed, especially in comparison to the sophisticated women at the party. She was wearing a simple black dress and black flats. She was exhausted from Ashley's whirlwind tour of the house, and she'd just had time to pull her hair back before the party started. She never wore much makeup, and she hadn't brought anything extra with her, so she just had to go as she was. She was certain she was the only person at the party who wasn't wearing spike heels and at least six layers of mascara.

"Are you joking?" said Jane, looking around at the other partygoers. "I stick out like a sore thumb."

"A lovely sore thumb," smiled Will. "They have to

work hard to be gorgeous," he said, gesturing towards the women around them, "for you, it's natural."

Jane blushed and looked away. Will's compliment was one of the nicest things that anyone had ever said to her.

"Well, I can't say that you blend," said Jane, trying to change the subject. "What on earth made you pick that outfit?"

Will smiled and looked down at his clothes. He was wearing a t-shirt that was emblazoned with a very fake looking tuxedo. A dressy sports coat, dark jeans, and a top hat completed his outfit.

"This is my party outfit," said Will, with a laugh. "I wear it to every party I attend. It helps make things more fun."

Jane shook her head and laughed. "I think you're going to have trouble at this party, despite the fake tuxedo. There's no chance of fun with this crowd."

"Ah, but that's where you're wrong," said Will suddenly, grabbing her arm. "We're going to make this party fun, despite having the odds stacked against us!"

"I don't see how that's possible," Jane replied.

"I have a lot of tricks up my sleeve," said Will. "Just wait! As long as you like to eat and dance, we'll be golden. This will be the best party you've ever been to!"

Will twisted his hand under his sleeve, and pulled out a rose, which he gave to Jane.

"Thank you," she said, in surprise. "I guess you really do have some tricks up your sleeve."

"That's just the beginning," replied Will. "But now let's get this party started! We're going to have the time of our lives tonight!"

"Alright," said Jane, skeptically. "But let's eat first, I'm starving!"

"A lady after my own heart!" said Will. "Food first, and then off to the dance floor!"

00001010

NEW LAB

Jane rolled over and opened her eyes slowly. She looked at the small clock on the bedside table and sat up with a start. It was 1:00 in the afternoon! She never slept that late! What were Remy and John going to think of her? They were supposed to start working in the lab today.

Jane hopped out of bed and hurriedly began getting ready. As she did so, she saw her clothes and shoes from the party last night in a heap on the floor. The party! She had almost forgotten. Of course, that's why she'd slept so late. She wasn't sure what time she'd gone to bed, but she knew it had been extremely late.

Jane smiled as she thought about the previous evening. It was probably the best time she'd ever had in her life. It all seemed so improbable. When she first got to the party, she was miserable. But then, once Will showed up, the entire night turned around. Will had been incredible. How had she never realized before how much fun he was?

Jane bent down to pull her shoes on and groaned. Her legs were so sore! She had danced almost the entire evening with Will. He was a pretty good dancer, but even better than that, he was totally comfortable on the dance floor and willing to do just about anything, even if he looked silly. He had put Jane completely at ease. Normally she would have felt uncomfortable dancing around so many wealthy people whom she didn't know. But with Will there, she didn't care. It had been so fun!

And then, to make the evening even more memorable, Will had sung a song for John and Ashley in honor of their engagement. Professor Chatham hadn't been exaggerating when he'd told her how talented Will was. He really could sing beautifully. After that, he'd done a short magic show, which wowed everyone in the crowd.

Jane shook her head. Will was certainly a man of many talents.

Just before leaving the room, Jane tried to tidy up a bit. She didn't want to leave the place a mess, despite what Remy had said about living in luxury.

Jane grabbed her dress from the night before. It was soaking wet.

"What on earth?" she said, before beginning to laugh. She had almost forgotten the best part. Somehow, Will had managed to convince everyone to jump into the pool with their clothes on, despite the fact that everyone was dressed in their finest. Jane had never seen that many soggy sequins and so much runny mascara in her life. It had been hilarious and so much fun. Everyone had enjoyed it, except maybe for Ashley.

"Upstaged by Will," laughed Jane to herself, "at her own engagement party."

It didn't get much better than that.

***

Jane hurried into the dining room, afraid that Remy and John had been waiting for her for hours.

However, when she entered the room, only John was there.

"Good morning sleepyhead," he said, with a smile. "I never realized you were such a partier!"

Jane blushed, feeling a little embarrassed by her

behavior at the party last night. Normally she was so serious. She never let herself go like that.

"Sorry," she said. "I didn't realize it either, until last night."

"It's nothing to be embarrassed about," smiled John. "It was nice to see you having so much fun."

Jane smiled slightly, and then, to change the subject said, "Well, I'm definitely not used to staying up so late. I hope you weren't waiting too long."

"I only got up about an hour ago," said John. "And I don't think Remy's awake yet. He stayed up much later than all of us. You know how hard he parties."

Jane grimaced. "Yes I do," she said. "Remy never does anything halfway."

"He probably won't be up for another hour or so," said John, "so we can take our time. I was just about to get some breakfast. Are you hungry?"

"Starving!" said Jane. "As usual!"

***

A few hours later, John, Jane, and Remy were on their way to the lab.

"Are you sure you're up for this today?" Jane asked Remy, as she looked at him more closely.

Remy was a disheveled mess. He was wearing a tattered pair of jeans and a button up shirt, which was buttoned incorrectly. His hair was rumpled and uncombed and his eyes were bloodshot. He had already consumed almost an entire pot of coffee on his own, but he looked as if he could use another pot.

"Huh?" grunted Remy. "Of course, why wouldn't I be? It's just a normal weekend."

Jane shook her head in disbelief. Apparently most of Remy's weekends were spent this way.

Remy shook himself, as if trying to wake up, and ran his fingers through his hair, making it even more of a mess. Then he said, excitedly, "Did you see how well the

RJ3's did at the party last night? I think they're going to make us the most money yet!"

John nodded in agreement. "Everyone was impressed. Did you check our stock this morning? It's skyrocketed! And we have more preorders for new RJ3's than we can fill in a year. It's incredible!"

"I knew those robots were winners," gloated Remy. "But just wait, it's going to get even better when we launch our humanoid robot. I can't wait!"

Jane half listened to John and Remy as they walked through the first floor of the mansion. She was happy for their success, but her mind was focused on other things. The more she thought about the humanoid robot, the more her presence at the mansion didn't make sense to her. When Remy talked about the robot, he made it sound as if it was already functional and almost finished. So, if that was true, then why did he need her help?

Even more pressing, Jane was confused about where exactly they were going. She had seen most of the mansion last night, but she still didn't know where the lab was. Remy was being very secretive about everything, as usual.

"Uh, guys," she asked finally, "where are we going?"

Remy smiled. "I'd tell you," he said, "but I'd have to kill you."

"I'm going to have to know at some point," said Jane. "So you might as well just tell me now. I'm pretty sure the lab can't be on the island though. I'm sure I would have seen it last night."

"You're right!" said Remy, laughingly. "There's no lab on this island."

"So," said Jane, her curiosity getting the best of her. "Where is it then?"

"Patience," said Remy. "You'll find out soon. But you need to remember this is top secret stuff. Not many people know about this lab. It's really just for me and

70

John to develop new products without any interference"

Remy and John continued walking, leading Jane through several more large rooms. Despite her best efforts, she was already turned around.

"This place is huge!" said Jane, in amazement.

"I know," said Remy. "I still get lost sometimes and I've lived here my entire life."

As Remy spoke, he turned abruptly down a narrow hallway. After several more turns, Remy stopped. They were standing in a small, dusty room that was filled with old furniture.

"Don't tell me this is the lab?" said Jane, incredulously.

Remy smiled at her mysteriously as he led the way towards the back of the room. "Maybe," he said.

"This is getting ridiculous," said Jane, beginning to think that Remy was playing some kind of joke on her. There was no way a state of the art computer research facility was going to be found in an old, unused storage room!

The three walked slowly to the back of the room. Remy pulled aside a tattered curtain and motioned for John and Jane to follow him. It was quite dark behind the curtain and it took a few moments for Jane's eyes to adjust to the dim lighting. When they did, she saw two of Remy's employees standing in front of a small door.

"Good afternoon Mr. Crofton," said the larger of the two. He was dressed in a suit and looked intimidating, but completely out of place in the dusty room.

"There'll be three of us," said Remy.

The second man put out his hand and held it motionless, palm up, in front of him. Remy waved his hand over the man's stationary palm. There was a soft beeping sound, and then the door before them slid open, revealing a sleek, modern elevator.

Jane looked at the man in disbelief. Did he just use

his own hand to scan Remy? Maybe her eyes were deceiving her? Suddenly, she felt as if she were in some strange science fiction movie.

"After you," said Remy, gesturing towards the elevator door.

Jane looked at Remy and John, speechless.

"Pretty cool, huh?" said John, smiling at Jane's discomfiture.

As soon as they were all in the elevator, the door closed noiselessly behind them and they began to descend rapidly.

"What just happened out there?" asked Jane.

"I thought you'd have noticed when you got on the boat yesterday," said Remy, with a proud smile. "You had to be positively identified to come over. It's our latest technology....totally non-invasive and seamless."

"But how does it work?" she asked.

"It'd take too long to explain now," said Remy, "but you'll know everything in good time. First, you have to see the lab! You're going to be blown away!"

Jane took a deep breath, trying to take it all in. She was still finding it hard to believe everything that she was seeing.

"So the lab is under the island?" she asked.

"Not quite," said John.

"It's actually on another island," said Remy. As he spoke, the elevator slowed to a stop and a door at the back slid open.

Before them was a platform and beyond that was a huge tunnel. At the end of the platform, there was a transparent partition, through which Jane could see what appeared to be an airlock. Inside the airlock, there was a very modern bullet train with a single car. Train tracks ran deep into the tunnel.

"Is this what I think it is?" asked Jane, in amazement.

"Oh yes!" replied Remy, his voice taut with excitement. "Evacuated Tube Transport, right here!"

"It's really just a prototype for ETT," explained John, modestly. "We're going to make it much better in the future. But basically, we bored a tunnel between the two islands and then sucked all the air out. Now, we can move much more quickly between the two islands because there isn't any air resistance."

"I understand how it works," interrupted Jane impatiently, "but I thought this technology was years away! What I want to know is how you did all of this? And in such a short amount of time?"

"Impressive, isn't it?" said Remy.

"Of course it is! But I don't see how any of this is possible," replied Jane.

"Patience . . . all will be revealed in time. You'll be able to see more when we get to the other side of the tunnel. Are you ready?" asked Remy, eagerly.

Jane took a deep breath, and said, "As ready as I'm going to be."

Remy led the way through the transparent doors to the airlock, which opened simultaneously with the doors to the train car. Once they were safely inside the car, both sets of doors silently shut behind them.

Jane gasped as she entered. It was just as luxurious as everything that she'd experienced so far, if not more so. It looked like the first class interior of a very expensive airline, or at least what Jane imagined first class would look like. She'd never flown first class in her life. Jane sat down gingerly on one of the plush chairs, unsure what to do with herself.

"We had to build the ETT in order to get to the other island," explained Remy, as he settled into one of the reclining chairs. "The water's too shallow and there are too many rocks to navigate safely by boat. That's what made it perfect for the lab. I wanted it to be completely inaccessible. Even getting there by helicopter is difficult. The wind currents that come off the island make it extremely dangerous to fly too close."

Jane nodded, her head in a whirl. This was crazy! She felt as if she was dreaming. Suddenly, the train lurched forward and Jane grabbed onto the edge of her seat. She didn't know why she was so nervous.

"Don't worry," said John, reassuringly, "it's a pretty smooth ride once we get going. It takes less than five minutes."

"Is Remy sleeping?" asked Jane, in surprise. She looked over at Remy, whose eyes were now closed.

"Remy always takes a power nap on the way over," said John.

"I don't know how he can sleep!" said Jane. "This is all so crazy!"

"I know it all seems incredible right now, but you'll get used to it," replied John, sympathetically.

Jane nodded again, still at a loss for words. She wasn't sure she wanted to get used to it.

Shortly after, the airlock door, which sealed the end of the tunnel, opened automatically, and they hurtled into the darkness.

***

A few minutes later, the train slid to a smooth stop and Remy jumped out of his seat, refreshed by his power nap.

"And we're here!" he shouted.

The train had reached the airlock at the other end of the tunnel. After a moment, the tunnel entrance was sealed and the air pressure equalized.

Remy grabbed Jane's arm and led her through the double door system of the train and the airlock. They were now standing on a platform similar to the one that they had just left.

"Right through here," said Remy, guiding Jane

74

towards a set of sliding glass doors that were inset into the rock face of the tunnel platform wall.

"Just wait," said Remy, "you're not going to believe your eyes!"

The doors slid open, and Jane entered the lab cautiously, as if she was walking off the edge of a gang plank. The shear scale of the lab was incredible. The interior was glisteningly clean and white. Long walkways ran between enormous glass cubes, where bustling robots were efficiently carrying out various tasks. In the center of the cavernous structure was a server farm that bristled with technology Jane had never seen before.

John looked over at Jane's astonished face and smiled. "A little better than the computer lab you're used to, huh?" he asked.

Jane nodded numbly. "I didn't know places like this existed," she said.

"They don't...except here!" said Remy. "When you have enough money you can do whatever you want. And this is exactly what I wanted. John and I have done all of our research and development here. This is how we've managed to accomplish so much."

Jane was still dumbfounded. With resources like this at her disposal, her work, which she had assumed was going to take years, could be completed in months.

"This is where you'll be working," said John, leading Jane over to a large array of computers in a secluded, glassed-in corner of the lab. "We set it up especially for you. There's more computing power here than you'll ever need ... and it's all right at your fingertips. Well, at least in a manner of speaking.

Jane followed John over to her new "office." The space had obviously been designed with her in mind. There were several of her favorite pictures already hanging on the wall and a small sectioned off enclosure, reserved for Bunnykins. And to her surprise, Bunnykins was happily hopping about, already quite at home in her new space.

"How on earth..." began Jane.

"We had one of the staff members bring her over while we were at breakfast," smiled John. "We wanted to surprise you...and Bunnykins!"

Jane nodded, speechless. She couldn't have designed the space better herself. It was perfect!

She looked from John to Remy, still at a loss for words. "I don't know what to say," she faltered. "This is going to change everything. I can finish my work...."

"Exactly," interrupted Remy, "work! That's why you're here. But, before you get started, you're going to need this!"

Remy held out a slim metal device towards Jane. She could tell it was a Brain Band, but smaller and more sleek.

"What is this?" asked Jane, suspiciously, as she took it from Remy.

"The latest and greatest Brain Band!" he said, proudly. "They're not even available to the general public yet. Rob tried to give you this on the yacht, remember? You're getting one of the prototypes. John and I programmed this one especially for you. Please take it this time...you're going to need it. It interfaces with everything in this space, the mainframe in the lab, and all of the service robots out on the main floor."

"Thanks," said Jane, trying to smile. "I'm sure it'll be great."

"Anyway," said Remy, "don't let us hold you back. If you want to get started now, feel free."

"You don't mind?" said Jane. She didn't want to be rude, but she was itching to get her hands on the machines in front of her.

"Mind?" laughed Remy. "We want you to work! We're as eager to see your finished research as you are!"

76

"But what about the work you want me to do…the simulations for your humanoid robot? Shouldn't I get started on those first?" asked Jane.

Remy waved his hand dismissively. "Don't worry about that right now," he said. "We'll have lots of time for simulations later. Anyway, working on your own research will help you get acclimated to the lab. It'll be good training for you."

Jane nodded, feeling just a bit nervous. She still didn't know why Remy was so interested in her work, but right now she wasn't going to worry about that. She had more important things to do.

"You don't mind being here by yourself?" asked John, who seemed as if he wanted an excuse to stay. "It can be a little creepy sometimes."

"No," smiled Jane, "I'm used to working alone. Plus I have Bunnykins here to keep me company. I'll be fine… don't worry."

"Alright," said John, "but if you need anything, all you have to do is contact us using your new Brain Band. All communications between us have been secured with several layers of digital cryptography. But the interface will be intuitive and transparent to you."

"Got it," said Jane.

"We'll be back in a few hours," said Remy, leading a reluctant John out of the lab. "We have our own work to do this afternoon."

Jane waved at the two and smiled. And then, as soon as they were gone, she seated herself eagerly at her access terminal. She had been regretting her decision to come to the island, but now, she wasn't so sure. This was an amazing opportunity. It would be crazy not to take advantage of it.

"I'm sure this won't last," said Jane to herself, "but while it does, I'm going to get as much of my own work done as I can."

Jane took the Brain Band that Remy had given her and looked at it for a long time. Then, she set it down on the desk and began orienting herself to the new technology that surrounded her.

00001011

TECHNOLOGY

Jane sighed and rubbed her head. It was her second day in the lab and she was feeling very frustrated. She'd only been working for about an hour, yet her eyes were already tired and aching.

"I don't want to waste another day," mumbled Jane to herself.

Her first day in the lab hadn't gone well. The technology that Remy and John had at their disposal was so much more advanced than anything she'd ever been exposed to. Jane hated to admit it, but she was having trouble figuring out how everything worked. Even worse, she couldn't get her VCS to interface with the advanced equipment in the lab, making it impossible for her to download her data from Malvern.

Jane sighed again and looked down at her desk. Her attention was immediately drawn to the Brain Band that Remy had given her the day before. It was still sitting there, unused. Jane didn't know why, but she was very reluctant to use it. She felt more comfortable with her own VCS, perhaps because it was untainted by Remy. But trying to work without it wasn't getting her anywhere.

"Doing things the old fashioned way doesn't seem to be working Bunnykins," said Jane thoughtfully, as she picked up the Brain Band and held it in her hand.

Just then, Jane felt a hand on her shoulder. She turned quickly, startled by the unexpected interruption.

"John! What are you doing here?" she said, smiling

in surprise. "I thought you and Remy had to work today."

John returned her smile. "I thought you might be having trouble settling in, so I came by to show you the interface and the lab."

"That would be nice," said Jane. "I could use a little help."

"How are things going?" asked John, curiously.

"A lot slower than they should be," replied Jane, with a blush. "I can't bring myself to try the new Brain Band. You know how I feel about them…"

"I don't like them either," said John, understandingly, "but to do any sort of computer work today you really need one, especially in here."

Jane nodded, reluctantly.

"I bet you don't even realize half the things it can do," continued John, with pride. "This newest model is really incredible. Let me show you…"

John trailed off as he started to interface with his Brain Band. Jane looked at him for a few moments, and then slowly slid her Brain Band on. Suddenly, she was jolted into what felt like another reality. John had connected to her Brain Band interface and was giving her a crash course on its new features. Connecting with John made Jane remember how well they worked together. It was as if the two were one mind, anticipating each other's thoughts and providing guidance when needed.

And, of course, John had been right. Jane could see now that the new Brain Band would make her work go hundreds of times faster. It allowed her to connect seamlessly with the mainframe computer in the lab. She could access the various system interfaces on demand and receive assistance from the service robots instantaneously.

"Wow!" said Jane. "I had no idea! I guess I should have put this on yesterday."

"It gets even better," smiled John. "Let me show you a few things around the lab."

John took Jane by the arm and led her towards the front of the vast space.

He stopped in front of a sectioned off area. There were several large metal work tables, covered with humanlike appendages. To Jane, it looked like the aftermath of a horrible massacre, an arm here, a foot there, part of leg, all randomly strewn about.

"What is this?" said Jane, her voice reflecting her horror at the scene.

John smiled at Jane's discomfiture. "Pick something up and take a look.

"That's okay," said Jane. "I'd rather not."

"No really," said John. "You have to look. Trust me."

With trepidation Jane walked over to the nearest table and picked up what appeared to be a human hand. As she looked at it more closely, her visual field was suddenly filled with a user interface that gave her access to detailed information about this particular hand. The design iteration number, name, and production date appeared above menus that offered even more in depth specs regarding its manufacture and design.

An overlay on the hand showed its internal parts, their connections, and dimensions. As Jane rotated the hand in front of her, the details changed to describe the components in the center of her visual field.

Jane was speechless. So this was Remy and John's humanoid robot, or at least a piece of it!

"As you can see, this is our main research and development lab for our next robot," said John, proudly. "Our goal is to make the most advanced, humanlike robot possible. We like to think of it as the first true humanoid robot for the mass market."

Jane nodded, still at a loss for words. This was well beyond any robotic technology she'd ever seen!

"When we get back to your office," continued John, "I'll show you how we use the mainframe to design, prototype, and manufacture our components. I wanted to show you the end result of our efforts first, so you could see just how complex and sophisticated our manufacturing processes are."

"That sounds great," said Jane, with a shiver, as she put the robot hand back onto one of the tables.

"Don't worry," laughed John, "we won't be building any hands or other body parts today. I have something in mind that you'll like much more. It's a little less complex, but it will work for demonstration purposes."

John led Jane back to her office. Jane was glad to get away from the humanoid robot enclosure. It was clear that Remy and John were conducting cutting edge research, but something about the humanoid robots made her very uncomfortable. She was intrigued and repelled at the same time.

"Here," said John, pulling up a chair in Jane's office, "have a seat." Jane sat down and John pulled up another chair, facing her.

"I'm accessing information from the mainframe, and projecting it into your visual field," said John. "In a moment, your interface will start demonstrating the algorithms that made all of this possible. It's a little tutorial I put together just for you. I think you're going to like it. It's some of the best programming I've ever done!"

As John spoke, an advanced simulation of his algorithm appeared in her visual field. Jane studied it for a moment and then gasped in surprise.

"It's learning as it goes!" said Jane.

"Exactly," said John. "I knew you'd see it right away. Not only does it adapt to new information and learn, but it can replicate itself, making small improvements with each new generation. It then shares those improvements to all of the other areas of the lab, so that every single piece of hardware can benefit."

"I've read about people trying to develop this type of technology," said Jane, "but I didn't think anyone had been successful yet."

"This type of technology has actually been in use for years," said John. "It just hasn't been used in the way that Remy and I have used it. Think about entertainment and social media companies trying to select content automatically for users in order to increase their advertising revenue. We've taken their content selection algorithms to the next level by advancing the machine learning algorithms to serve our own manufacturing needs."

Jane nodded thoughtfully. "So your algorithms figure out the best, most efficient way to do things?"

"Exactly!" said John. "We use the algorithm to simulate all of the possible hardware and software configurations in at least a billion different ways until optimization is achieved. It's saved us years of development time on our robots and other technology, like the Brain Band. It's also allowed us to optimize the design of the boring machine which built the tunnels under the islands, the ETT system, the lab, and even your office."

"I didn't see how it was possible that you could accomplish so much in only five years," said Jane. "But using your algorithms and adaptive manufacturing techniques..." she trailed off.

John smiled. "With learning and improving algorithms like mine, everything is sped up by years!"

"But," said Jane thoughtfully, "how can you be sure that your algorithm is actually improving itself all the time?"

"What do you mean?" asked John.

"What gives you certainty that the changes your

algorithm is making are actually improvements?" asked Jane. "Just because something is faster and more efficient doesn't necessarily mean it's better."

"Well..." said John, hesitantly, "it's obviously getting better each time! Just look around you!"

Jane nodded, but didn't say anything. She was impressed with John's work, but a bit scared by it too. She could see Remy's influence. Remy was always rushing ahead in order to market the next great piece of technology, without thinking about the potential consequences of his actions.

"Anyway, this is actually what I really wanted to show you!" said John, grabbing Jane by the hand again and pulling her up from her chair.

John led Jane to the back wall of her office. They looked through the glass wall into another large glassed-in space, in which Jane could see thousands of small robots swarming about.

"Are those what I think they are?" asked Jane, wonderingly.

"Yes!" smiled John. "Nanobots! We have millions of them! It's a project we nicknamed SWARM. Remy and I have programmed them to work together in order to turn raw materials into finished projects. Using my algorithms, we can optimize them to work in the most efficient and quickest way possible."

"They're amazing!" said Jane, captivated by the swarm of robots coordinating and collaborating before her eyes.

"I'm going to have them build something so you can really see how incredible they are!" said John, as he began interfacing with his Brain Band.

As if on cue, all of the nanobots stopped what they were doing. As soon as the nanobots were still, John opened an access panel on the back wall of Jane's office.

"You're going to love this!" he said, excitedly.

A group of nanobots trooped out of their glass enclosure and through the access panel into Jane's office. They were still for a few moments. Then, almost as one, they began moving again, each nanobot coordinating with the other to finish their new task.

Jane watched for a moment and then laughed in delight. "They're rebuilding Bunnykins' enclosure!"

"Exactly!" said John.

"But how are they doing it so perfectly?" asked Jane, curiously. "This one looks even better than the first one!"

"We built the first one using publically available information about the Holland Lop breed," said John, as he watched the nanobots with pride. "But this one is being built using information gathered from Bunnykins' actual use of the space. The mainframe computer determined Bunnykins' preferences by observations it gathered when she was in the enclosure yesterday. The available space for the enclosure was computed using the dimensions of your office and finally, using AI, the optimum design was determined after millions of simulations were run."

"Incredible," said Jane, fascinated by the scurrying swarm in front of her.

"In about thirty more seconds, they'll be done!" said John.

Jane looked at the nanobots rushing about. In a few seconds, they stopped moving. And, there, before her eyes, was a new, improved enclosure for Bunnykins. The entire process had taken only a few minutes.

Jane shook her head in disbelief, "I didn't think things like this were possible."

"They are!" said John. "At least for RJ Robotics!"

***

A little while later, Jane was alone in the lab again. Her head was whirling with everything she had seen.

This was technology that had only been written about or speculated upon. It was still the stuff of science fiction novels. But here she was, seeing it all with her own eyes. She didn't know whether to feel excited or terrified. It was clear that John and Remy had rushed things, going far beyond the safety threshold in their use of new technology. But what could she say? Remy had never listened to her in the past, and John was completely under Remy's thumb. Plus, what basis did she have for her objections to what they were doing? It's not as if she'd seen evidence of anything harmful.

Jane shook her head in dismay. Things were so much simpler back at Malvern. There, everything was black and white. Here, she didn't know what was right or wrong.

00001100

HAUNTED

"I can't believe we're so late!" said Jane, as she and John rushed down the hall towards the lab.

They were supposed to have met Remy hours ago, but John's car had broken down on their way to the college.

"Remy's going to be mad," said John. "We're already behind on the project as it is."

"I know," said Jane, "but this isn't something that we can rush. What's the worst that happens anyway? We don't win the contest? Who cares! We'll still have done some amazing research!"

John shook his head. "You don't know Remy!"

Jane slowed down, looking at the numbered doors in the hallway.

"I still don't know why he wanted to meet in the animal lab," said Jane, pausing in front of the last door at the end of the hallway. "It's not like we need anything in here. We're not ready to start scanning yet."

Jane pushed the door to the computer lab open and froze in horror.

There, before her, were Remy and Ashley. Remy was sitting at one of the lab tables, holding a scanner. Ashley was perched on the edge of the table, snacking on a bag of popcorn. They were surrounded by dead animals.

Ashley looked up. "Hi there," she laughed, gleefully. "You missed the show! This is way better than the movies!"

"What are you doing?" whispered Jane, overcome with repulsion at the sight that met her eyes.

Remy stood up from the chair where he was sitting, walking over to them a bit unsteadily.

"We're doing research!" he said. "And getting ready to win that contest!"

"Are you drunk?" asked Jane, indignantly.

"Drunk?" laughed Remy. "I'm never drunk."

As Remy spoke, he waved a metal instrument in the air above his head.

"Is that my scanner?" asked Jane. "Please don't tell me you've been using it on the animals. It's not ready."

"Of course we've been using it!" said Remy. "What else would we do with it!? We can't figure out how to get it to work if we don't test it!"

"Do another one!" said Ashely, eagerly. "They have to see this thing in action."

"For you my dear, anything," said Remy, with a mock bow.

He turned and staggered back to the table.

"Would you like to do the honors?" asked Remy, looking at Ashley.

"Don't mind if I do," laughed Ashley, as she walked towards the row of animal cages that lined the back wall of the room.

"I think we might be almost out," she said. "But wait! There's one left. This little rodent will do nicely."

Ashley opened the last cage in the row and grabbed a small rabbit by its ears. The rabbit squealed in protest, which only made Ashley laugh harder.

"I don't think it likes me!" she giggled, as she plopped the rabbit down on the table in front of Remy.

"Now watch this," said Remy, holding up the scanner dramatically. "You are not going to believe your eyes!"

Jane had been watching the entire scene unfold

before her in horror. She looked over at John, who hadn't said anything yet.

Finally, John mumbled weakly, "Hey Remy, do you really think this is a good idea? Maybe we should stop…."

"What!" interrupted Remy, "and ruin all the fun! No way! I want you and Jane to see this. It's unbelievable!"

Jane looked towards John, but he wouldn't meet her eyes. Jane's face fell. John wasn't going to do anything. He wasn't going to stop Remy.

Remy held the scanner towards the rabbit's head, and the helpless animal squealed in pain.

She couldn't let this happen. If John wouldn't stop Remy she would.

Jane ran over to the table and grabbed Remy's arm. The two struggled for a few moments with the scanner, pulling and pushing it over the rabbit's head. Finally, Jane overpowered him and grabbed the scanner.

Before Remy could stop her, she smashed it on the floor.

"That's it!" she shouted. "We're done!"

Remy seemed to grow in size before her, looking monstrous and evil.

"Oh no we're not!" he said, holding up another scanner before her.

Before she could do anything, he'd jabbed the scanner into the rabbit's head.

Then, he turned towards her. "You're next," he said.

Jane screamed, but it was too late.

***

Jane awoke with a start. Her heart was pounding and she was sweating. She hadn't had this nightmare in years. But, after two days in Remy and John's lab, she was reliving the horrors of the past in her dreams. To make matters worse, instead of the dream ending where it had in real life, with the destruction of the scanner, it continued, with Remy killing Bunnykins and her.

Jane tried to quiet her breathing and calm down. "It was just a bad dream," she said to herself. "It wasn't real."

She switched on the light on the bedside table and looked down on the floor next to her bed. Bunnykins was sleeping quietly in her carrier. She was alive and well.

Jane sighed in relief. She didn't know what she had been expecting, but it was reassuring to see Bunnykins looking so peaceful.

"This place must be getting to me," she said, her forehead creased in worry. "Maybe John was right about the lab being creepy."

It was only Sunday night. Jane still had almost a week left on the island. But, if her bad dreams continued, she wasn't sure she was going to be able to make it.

00001101

SOMETHING AMISS

Jane sighed in frustration. She was tired from her sleepless, nightmare haunted night. And now, to make matters worse, her Brain Band wasn't functioning properly.

John's instructions on how to use the new Brain Band had allowed Jane to start downloading her data from Malvern the previous day. But now, there seemed to be some type of error. Her download was stuck.

"Too much technology," muttered Jane to herself. She suspected that the Brain Band she was using was a bit too advanced for Malvern's antiquated equipment to handle.

She'd just have to keep trying, and hope that she didn't waste too much time. There was just so much to do! Despite the dramatic increase in computing power at her disposal, Jane was beginning to feel overwhelmed by the long list of tasks that she needed to accomplish.

First, she had to transfer all of her data to the new lab. This included all of the partitions of Bunnykins' brain scan prior to her injury and the ones completed after her brain had healed. But even this was proving to be more difficult than she'd planned. Once the transfer was complete, she needed to stitch all of the data back together and check it for errors. Jane wasn't exactly sure how she was going to do this, but she was hoping the inspiration would come when needed. Only then could she start transforming the raw data into useful code and begin her search for the subroutines that she had always postulated were responsible for brain healing and repair. Jane's theory was that these subroutines were similar in all mammals. If this proved to be true, her research could be used to help repair and heal traumatic brain injuries in humans.

And all of this thanks to the amazing creature hopping about in the new, improved enclosure right beside her. Jane looked at Bunnykins and smiled slightly. Then, she looked around the lab and sighed again. Despite her best intentions, she was feeling anxious and on edge.

"What's wrong with me?" she said to herself. "I have an entire state of the art lab to myself. This is just what I wanted! Or what I thought I wanted..."

Jane wasn't sure what was bothering her, but she was finding it very hard to stay focused on her work. Her thoughts kept wandering, eventually leading her back to the nightmares she'd had the previous evening.

"At least I have you to keep me company," Jane said to Bunnykins. "We'll get through this together."

Jane adjusted a few of the settings on her Brain Band and tried to restart her data transfer from Malvern. This time she was successful! Finally, she'd be able to get some work done.

As Jane's data downloaded , she received a prompt in her visual field.

"This data already exists, would you like to replace it?" read the prompt.

"What?" said Jane to herself. "That's not possible!"

Jane scrolled through the files listed in her visual field. As she reached the last set of folders, she realized that the Brain Band prompt was correct. All of her data was already on the lab computer, including her notes on the machine, Bunnykins neural pathway data, and every other file that she'd ever saved on her computer at

Malvern.

Jane was aghast. She'd never shared her work with anyone else. She had assumed it was securely stored on the Malvern University computer system. Had Remy and John been spying on her?

Jane tried to access the origins of the data files, but there was no information available. Whoever had downloaded her files hadn't left an obvious trail. There were no transfer dates, making it impossible for Jane to tell when the files were copied.

"What is going on?" muttered Jane. The discovery of her pilfered files had increased the anxiety she was already feeling.

There's just something off about everything here… the lab, Remy, the mansion…nothing feels right," mumbled Jane to herself.

As she spoke, Jane looked over at Bunnykins again, who suddenly seemed very agitated. She was hopping against the walls of her enclosure, as if she wanted to get out.

"You seem as nervous as I do," she said, looking at the rabbit in concern.

"I wonder…" said Jane, gazing curiously at Bunnykins.

Jane lifted Bunnykins out of the enclosure and set her down on the office floor.

"Alright Bunnykins," she said. "I know you feel it too. There's something wrong here. Why don't you show me what it is?"

Bunnykins lifted her head, as if sniffing the air, and then hopped leisurely to the office door. Jane opened the glass door for her, expecting the rabbit to hop slowly out and into the lab. However, to Jane's horror, Bunnykins scampered quickly through the door, around a corner, and then out of sight.

Jane felt the panic rise in her throat. She ran

frantically out into the lab, trying to catch up with Bunnykins. But she had no idea where the rabbit was or which way she had gone.

Jane hadn't expected Bunnykins to run away. She had never acted like that before. But Jane could see now that releasing her small pet into the lab was a terrible mistake! The entire lab was filled with potentially dangerous equipment. And there were service robots everywhere. Bunnykins could be injured or killed!

Jane ran down the far side of the lab where her office was located, peering into one transparent cubicle after another on her way. But there was no sign of Bunnykins.

"What have I done?" said Jane, almost in despair.

Just as she was about to give up hope, she caught a flash of movement out of the corner of her eye. Jane whirled around, just in time to see Bunnykins hopping rapidly away, down another row of cubicles. Jane ran after her as quickly as she could.

When Jane reached the end of the row, she sighed in relief. There was Bunnykins, sitting patiently, as if waiting for her to catch up. As she approached, Bunnykins started hopping forward quickly, staying just out of her reach.

"Not without me!" said Jane, as she ran after the rabbit, trying to get close enough to scoop her up.

Bunnykins hopped rapidly towards the back wall of the lab, with Jane in close pursuit. When she reached the wall, Bunnykins stopped for a moment and looked back towards Jane.

"Thank goodness," said Jane. "We hit a dead end."

But Bunnykins seemed undeterred. She sniffed at the wall a few times, and then, suddenly, she hopped forward and disappeared. Jane gasped. What had just happened?

Jane put her hand out to touch the wall. To her

surprise, her hand passed right through it.

"What the . . .?!" said Jane, pulling her hand back in shock.

To Jane, the wall looked completely normal…solid and well built. There was nothing to indicate anything out of the ordinary. But, after staring at the wall for a moment, Jane suddenly realized what was happening. She pulled off her "improved" Brain Band and the wall disappeared, as if it had never existed. It had been a projection from the Brain Band onto her visual field.

Jane shook her head in disbelief. "What is going on?" she said to herself.

Jane walked into the room, which only moments before had been completely hidden from view. Bunnykins, who was waiting near where the wall used to be, looked up at her eagerly. Jane scooped up the rabbit and hugged her tightly.

"Never do that again!" she admonished the rabbit, giving her another hug.

Then, Jane began examining her surroundings more closely.

"Why didn't they want me to see this Bunnykins?" she said. "I don't even know what half of this stuff is…."

Jane trailed off. She was standing in the middle of the room, in front of a giant piece of technology that was clearly the centerpiece of the hidden lab. It was her brain scanning machine! The machine that she had designed but hadn't even started to build yet! She had dreamed about it so many times, but it had only existed in her mind. But now, here it was…completely finished.

Remy and John had somehow managed to build her machine. But how? And why?

As Jane walked slowly around the huge device, she was amazed at how closely it matched her plans, even down to tiny, seemingly unimportant details. Every specification that she had ever committed to her notes was built into the machine. Even some of her earliest safety features, including biometric activation protocols from her very first sketches of the machine, were there.

"Everything's exactly as I planned," she said, in amazement.

However, as Jane examined the machine more closely, she noticed a few differences. The small control panel that she had planned was gone, most likely replaced by a Brain Band interface. And the scanning area, which was enclosed in a clear polycarbonate material, was much larger than her original plans had indicated. Her machine was only intended for small mammals. But this machine looked as if it was large enough to scan human beings.

"What are they up to?" she whispered to herself.

***

Jane walked slowly back towards her office, still in shock. She couldn't believe what she had just seen. Her machine....complete! Her mind was racing. Remy and John must have hacked into the college computer system. It was the only explanation. But when? Had they been spying on her for a long time, or was this a new development? And more importantly, why? Why would Remy and John be interested in building her machine? And why had they made changes to it? None of it made any sense.

Even more worrying to Jane, it had been relatively easy for her to find the secret lab and her machine. Had they wanted her to find it? What kind of game was Remy playing?

Jane sat down in her office, setting Bunnykins in her lap.

"What do they want?" asked Jane.

Jane put her Brain Band back on and began interfacing with the lab computer. If John and Remy had been hacking into the system at Malvern and following her research, she knew how to find out. She was just as good a forensic computer scientist as they were, if not better. She would be able to see exactly what they'd been up to.

00001110

DISCOVERY

"I found the machine!" said Jane, her voice tense.

Jane had just burst into the library, where John and Remy were sitting, enjoying a few drinks before dinner. She was now standing in front of the two, looking at them angrily.

"Oh Jane!" said Remy. "Why do you always have to be so dramatic? Can't you walk into a room like a normal person and have a civilized conversation? Why don't you take a seat and have a drink? John makes a mean cocktail…"

Jane interrupted. "I don't want to sit . . . and I don't want a drink. What I want is an explanation."

"You make my head hurt," sighed Remy. "Why don't you tell her John? I don't want to get a migraine."

John looked at Remy in surprise. "You want me to explain?" he asked.

"I just don't have it in me tonight," said Remy. "But tell her the short version. I'm hungry and I don't want to wait too long to eat dinner."

John nodded at Remy and then looked at Jane nervously. "I suppose we owe you an apology."

"Of course you do!" said Jane. "But what I want first is an explanation! Why did you build my machine? And how long have you been spying on me?"

"So I guess you know how we did it already?" asked John.

"Yes," said Jane, impatiently. "Any idiot with a 2-year

degree in computer science could follow your hacking. It's pathetic! I should have noticed, but it never occurred to me that anyone would be interested enough in my research to hack into my computer."

"We're sorry about that," said John. "I guess there were better ways to go about it."

"But your password was Bunnykins after all!" added Remy. "If you didn't want people hacking into your computer you should have picked something a little more difficult. You made it much too easy for us!"

"So it's my fault that you were spying on me?" said Jane, in disbelief. Remy's outlook on the world made no sense to her.

"How long has this been going on?" she asked.

"Not that long, said John, looking embarrassed. "Maybe six months at the most."

Jane shook her head, angrily. She could tell that John was lying. For all she knew, they could have been spying on her for the last five years. But she had more important questions to answer at the moment.

"But why?" demanded Jane. "What are you two up to?"

John looked over at Remy who nodded again. He cleared his throat nervously and then began speaking, "It's sort of our idea of a surprise. Perhaps we didn't go about it in the best way, but we wanted to surprise you. We knew you'd figure out the wall was a projection pretty quickly. But we wanted you to! We thought that walking through the wall would be like unwrapping a gift. It's our way of making up to you for what happened."

Jane looked from John to Remy, incredulous. "You did all of this as an apology?"

"We both treated you terribly at Malvern," said John. "We wanted to do something to make things right again."

Jane shook her head unbelievingly and looked

directly at Remy. "That's a nice story, but I don't believe it."

"You have to," said John. "It's the truth."

"Alright," said Jane, skeptically. "Then if you just built the machine for me, why did you make changes to it? I assume it's controlled by a Brain Band interface. And you made it big enough to scan people! That wasn't in my original plans!"

"Jane," said Remy, impatiently. "Get with the times! No one does anything without a Brain Band anymore! You're living in the past if you believe that."

"And, we're not responsible for the changes to the scanner," said John. "It was the nanobots! They built the machine using your plans and my efficiency algorithm. You made mention in your notes of eventually building another machine that could scan people. The nanobots had access to that information. It would have been inefficient for them to build two machines. So they just built one that could scan small mammals and people too. It's actually a really awesome system. The scanning bed is totally automated and will adjust based on whatever you're trying to scan."

Jane nodded thoughtfully. John and Remy's answers to her questions made sense. Maybe there was some truth in what they were saying. But there was still a major obstacle....Remy.

"No matter what you say, I don't trust you, Remy," said Jane.

"That's probably smart of you," smiled Remy. "I don't trust anyone!"

"I'm serious," replied Jane. "I don't know what you're up to, but you're not the kind of person who does things to apologize."

"Jane," said Remy, "people can change. I'm really not as bad as you think. I do nice things sometimes."

Jane looked at Remy, unconvinced.

"And John can be pretty persuasive," added Remy. "It was his idea."

"That sounds more like it," she said, as she sank into a chair across from the two.

Jane felt some of the anxiety she'd been feeling begin to dissipate. She knew that Remy wasn't telling the entire truth, but she also knew that John was sincere in his protestations of the machine being a gift for her. He wasn't lying about that. Of course, she knew she couldn't trust Remy, no matter what he said. For him, there was always an ulterior motive. But for now, she could try to make the best of things and proceed with caution.

"So I guess you brought me here under false pretenses?" said Jane. "You don't really need my help with your humanoid robot."

Remy laughed. "Bingo!" he said. I wasn't sure how long it would take you to figure that one out. Of course, we'd love to have your help with any of RJ Robotics projects, but our humanoid robots are under control."

John blushed, "We're sorry we had to tell a few lies to get you here. But we didn't think there was any other way to convince you."

"There probably wasn't," said Jane. She was silent for a moment, lost in thought. It was still hard to comprehend everything that had happened that afternoon.

"So," asked Remy, expectantly, "are you excited?"

"You have to be!" said John, with a smile.

Jane smiled back at John and then sat silently for a few more minutes. "I think I'm still in shock. That machine has existed in my head for years. I don't think I really believed it would ever be built."

"Well, it's definitely real!" said Remy. "We built it using your plans and your research."

"I know," said Jane. "I guess I should say thank you…

to both of you."

Remy waved his hand. "No thank you's necessary! We had fun building it!"

"It's the very least we could do," said John. "I know it doesn't make up for everything, but it's a start."

Jane shook her head, still in disbelief. "I was feeling overwhelmed this morning by all of the work that I still had to do. Of course, having access to your lab speeds things up…but having access to my machine! If it works correctly, the machine and your mainframe are capable of scanning and processing brain data almost instantaneously. It turns a very long, multistep process into one simple step. It's going to change everything!"

John smiled at Jane's excitement. "We know. And you don't have to worry…the machine will work perfectly. We want you to be able to finish your research."

"We want to help too, if you don't mind," added Remy. "That machine is fascinating! We built it, but I still don't really understand how it works."

"You haven't tried to use it, I hope!" said Jane.

It hadn't occurred to her until now that John and Remy might have been experimenting with her machine. There was a testing phase that needed to be completed before the machine was safe to use. But if they had!? She didn't even want to think about it.

"No," said John reassuringly, "of course not. We know the machine needs to be tested first. We read all of your notes. Plus, we can't get it to work without you. You left that part of your research a bit vague."

"On purpose," said Jane, with relief.

"So you'll let us help you?" asked Remy. "It'll be fun to be working together again!"

"On one condition," said Jane.

Remy groaned. "There's always conditions with you."

"I'm the only one who gets to use the machine," said

Jane, firmly.

John nodded his head. "That's fine with me. It is your machine after all. You should have control over it."

Remy rolled his eyes. He hated not being in charge. However, after a moment, he shrugged his shoulders and said, "Fine...whatever you want. As long as we get to work together, I'm good."

Before Jane could respond, she was interrupted by Ashley, who barged into the room and slammed the door dramatically behind her.

"What are you all doing in here?" said Ashley, looking at the three in annoyance. "Isn't it time to eat dinner? I'm dying of hunger!"

"Sorry, dear," said John, as he got up from his chair to greet her. "We can eat now. We were talking about work and lost track of the time."

Ashley glared at John and stalked across the room, plopping herself down on the couch next to Remy. She grabbed a handful of pretzels from a bowl on the table.

"You know I don't like to be kept waiting," she muttered, as she began crunching angrily on the pretzels.

John whispered to Jane, "She's not usually like this. She turns into a different person when she's hungry."

Jane didn't see much of a difference between hungry Ashley and regular Ashley, but she nodded her head understandingly anyway.

Just then, there was a gentle knock at the door and one of Remy's household staff entered the room slowly. The man looked around vaguely, before focusing his attention on Remy.

"Dinner is served in the dining room," he announced, solemnly. Then, he turned around slowly and left the room.

Ashley stared at the man in amazement and then burst out laughing uproariously.

"Did you do that?" she asked Remy. "It's incredible! Dinner is served!" she said, in a deep tone of voice, mimicking the man who had just left the room.

"Now Ashely," said Remy, with a warning glance at his sister. "Control yourself….we don't want to be rude."

Ashely tried to stifle her laughter, but with no success. "I can't," she snorted. "It's just too funny!"

Jane glanced at John for an explanation, but he only shrugged his shoulders.

"She gets this way sometimes," he said. "I have no idea why."

Jane looked at Ashley, who was still laughing uncontrollably. The man who had announced dinner was certainly strange. But he wasn't that different from the rest of the household staff. What was wrong with Ashley?

Finally, Ashley's laughter subsided and she tripped over to John.

"Let's go eat, Johnny!" she said, taking him by the arm.

"I hope there's lots of meat tonight!" she added gleefully, with a pointed glance at Jane. "I could eat a whole cow! Hahaha! Or maybe three or four rabbits! They do make a tasty little meal!"

00001111

ROBO-BUNNY

"We have one more surprise for you," said John, excitedly.

It was the next day, and Jane, Remy, and John were in the lab together, getting ready to test Jane's machine.

Jane groaned, "I don't think I can deal with another surprise," she said. "The machine was enough!"

"You're going to like this one!" said Remy. "It was my idea, so it's awesome."

"One moment," said John dramatically. He walked over to a set of cabinets and removed a small box.

"Close your eyes!" said Remy. "It'll make the surprise better!"

Jane sighed and did as she was told.

"Okay," said John, "you can open them now!"

Jane opened her eyes. There, on the floor before her was a small rabbit. It looked exactly like Bunnykins!

Jane looked over at John, who was busy interfacing with his Brain Band, clearly controlling the rabbit. As Jane watched, the rabbit hopped about on the floor, moving like a normal, living creature.

"Meet Robo-bunny!" said John.

"How did you do that?" asked Jane, in amazement.

"We were hoping you'd mistake it for Bunnykins," said Remy.

"There's only one Bunnykins," smiled Jane. "But this rabbit is pretty convincing. It looks so real!"

"It's just about as close to real as you can get!" said

Remy, as he watched the rabbit with delight. "We modeled it using Bunnykins brain scan."

"Oh!" said Jane in surprise. "I forgot that you had access to all of Bunnykins' data! I guess you've started to analyze it?"

"You could say that," laughed Remy. "We're actually done!"

"What?!" said Jane, shocked. "I've been working on analyzing Bunnykins brain scan for almost five years and I've barely scratched the surface. Just getting the data into the computer without crashing all of the systems took years!"

"You don't have our systems," said Remy. "And you don't have John!"

"I didn't have that much to do with it," said John, modestly. "It's mainly because we have so much computing power. It makes analyzing the data simple."

"Don't be so humble!" said Remy. "Once we got all of Bunnykins data into the computer, John created an amazing algorithm that translates mammalian neural connections into useable robotic subroutines. He optimized it for speed, then the mainframe optimized those routines into functional hardware, concentrating on the subroutines for movement and behavior. Last but not least, SWARM took care of Robo-bunny's construction just before our arrival this morning."

"I guess there's a reason we used to call you the King of Algorithms back in college," Jane smiled. "I wish I'd had you at Malvern with me over the past five years. I'd be much further along!"

John blushed, obviously embarrassed by all of the praise. "It was really nothing," he said.

"I'll be the judge of that," replied Jane. "Can I see your work? I've been poring over this data for years, with nothing to show for it. It'd be amazing to see what you've done."

108

"Of course," smiled John. "I'd love to show you."

Jane sat down next to John. They connected via Brain Band, and John began to show her the work he had done.

"When I first saw the data on Bunnykins scan, I realized that it was fragmented due to the limitations of the systems at Malvern," said John.

"You're right," sighed Jane. "I have no other way to gather the data, except in small subsets. I can only store a small portion of the scan in the limited amount of RAM on the system in my office. Each time I did a scan, I filled the system memory and then offloaded that data to the campus mainframe. It was an extremely inefficient process, but I needed to ensure that there was sufficient overlap in the scans to be able to stitch it all back together someday… if I ever received enough funding to upgrade the system to store and process the data in one location. I didn't think I'd ever finish at the rate I was going. The daily scans and the nightly uploads were taking forever. And every few days the connections would break, or the office system would crash, causing me to lose that day's work. I'd have to come in early, reboot everything, and start over again."

John smiled. "Well you don't have to worry about that anymore. Look at this…once we got all of Bunnykins scans, the algorithm went to work recognizing the redundant data at the end of each file and at the start of the next. It glued all of the pieces back together and created this neural pathway simulation. You should be able to see the virtualized simulation in your field of view," said John.

Jane was silent for several moments as she studied the neural pathway simulation that John had created from Bunnykins' brain scans.

"Incredible!" she breathed, in awe. "I had no idea how I was going to stitch all of Bunnykins' data back together and still have it make sense. But you've done it perfectly! And, with your simulation, I can scroll through the data and see all of the connections visually. That makes it so much easier to understand…and it will be so much easier to search through!"

"I thought you'd appreciate that!" said John. "Anyway, in terms of Robo-bunny, we used all of the information from the neural pathway simulation to create an exact replica of Bunnykins' brain. Then, we implanted it in a robot that looks very much like her. The only difference from the real thing is that you can control this one with your Brain Band."

"That's very impressive," said Jane, thoughtfully, as she reluctantly turned her attention from the neural scan to look over at Robo-bunny. "But your bunny does leave a bit to be desired. Pets are interesting because they have minds of their own…it makes interacting with them unpredictable and fun."

"If you leave the bunny in fully autonomous mode, it will act exactly like a real rabbit," explained John. "But you have the added benefit of being able to protect it from danger, or turn it off when you're bored with it."

"I still prefer the real thing!" said Jane.

She was silent for a moment as she watched Robo-bunny hop about on the floor. "I guess you took my work in another direction. My goal is to find the neural pathways from Bunnykins that are related to healing, not the pathways for movement and behavior."

"What's the point of that?" said Remy.

"Well," said Jane, surprised at Remy's reaction, "those healing pathways could prove to be very valuable! If we can identify them, they can be used in other applications, like healing human brain damage."

Remy waved his hand dismissively. "That's a waste of time! You can't sell a cure! But you can sell other things…"

"Like toy bunnies," said Jane, dryly.

"Exactly!" said Remy. "Now you're thinking like me! I don't think you realize the full potential of your research. We could use your machine to find all sorts of other, more useful neural pathways. We could find marketable algorithms that would make us millions, like…"

"That's not what my machine is for," interrupted Jane.

"You have no vision!" said Remy, impatiently. "But let's not argue about that right now. Let's get back to the real reason we're here. We need to get this machine up and running!"

"It's not going to be that simple," replied Jane. She got up from where she was sitting and walked over to the machine. "You did an amazing job building my machine, but there are a few things that you got wrong. I'm going to have to fix them."

"Ugh," groaned Remy, "more delays!"

"It won't take that long," said Jane, "but you need to be patient. This is a very complicated machine. Everything needs to be working perfectly before we start testing."

"Alright," said Remy, reluctantly. "We'll leave you alone to fix the machine. I have work to do for RJ Robotics anyway. And Johnny here has wedding planning to do with Ashely!"

John started and his face reddened. "Oh no!" he said. "I completely forgot! We're supposed to meet with the wedding planner this afternoon. If I don't hurry I'm going to be late."

"Ashley doesn't like to be kept waiting," laughed Remy. "We'll come check on you later," he added. "Hopefully you'll have something to show us."

Jane waited until the two left, and then walked over to Robo-bunny. Using her Brain Band, she deactivated the robot.

"You're pretty amazing," she said to the rabbit, who hopped one last time and then went still. "But, for some reason, you creep me out!"

Jane picked up Robo-bunny and put it back in its box. Then she walked over to her machine. She stood in front of it for a long time, lost in her own thoughts.

Then she sighed. "Time to get to work," she said to herself.

00010000

SCANNING

The next morning, Jane was ready for Remy and John. She had spent hours in the lab the previous day, calibrating the machine to get it ready for testing. She had even used the nanobots, deploying SWARM to make revisions and corrections to the machine.

Even more importantly, Jane had finally found some time to work on her own research. With the help of John's algorithm, Jane had parsed Bunnykins' entire brain scan visually. After careful examination, she had identified several interesting pathways that seemed promising in her search for healing and repair subroutines. She was now running the subroutines in simulations on the mainframe, and hoped to have her first results by the end of the day.

Jane had made significant progress, but she didn't feel happy.

She looked down at Bunnykins, who was sleeping peacefully in her lap.

"I don't know about you Bunnykins," said Jane, "but as amazing as all of this is, I still prefer the lab at Malvern."

Jane sighed as she stroked the sleeping rabbit. Everything had been happening so fast. She was still having trouble taking it all in.

"I wish I was more excited," said Jane, to herself, "but right now I just feel worn out."

Jane still wasn't sleeping well. Vague nightmares

continued to disturb her sleep. They weren't as vivid as when she had first arrived at the mansion, but they were still there.

"A few more days and we'll be back home," said Jane, "I promise."

***

"Wake up!" shouted Remy, with a laugh. "Sleeping on the job already?"

Jane started. She must have fallen asleep while she was waiting for Remy and John.

Jane smiled and rubbed her eyes. "Sorry," she said. "You two are slave drivers."

"We're not slave drivers," said Remy. "If you came to work for us, you wouldn't think so. You'd be living in luxury."

"We really could use someone like you at RJ Robotics," added John. "I always thought the three of us made an incredible team."

"We'll get Jane to change her mind," said Remy, confidently. "Once she sees this machine in action I know she's going to want to stay!"

"We'll see," said Jane. "It's time we got to work though."

Jane stood up and stretched. She looked around for Bunnykins, who was no longer on her lap. She must have hopped away when she heard Remy and John enter the lab. Bunnykins had an aversion to Remy and usually fled whenever he appeared. Jane looked under her desk, and there was Bunnykins, sitting very quietly, clearly hiding from Remy.

"I don't blame you," said Jane softly to the rabbit.

"Are we finally ready to do some testing?" asked John.

"If you're up for it," said Jane.

"I don't think I can wait any longer!" replied John, eagerly.

"Why don't we do a 'dress rehearsal' first?" suggested Remy. "We can do everything that we'd do if we were going to scan a real subject, except for the actual scan. That way we'll make sure we all know what we're doing."

"That sounds like a good start," said Jane. "Who wants to be the guinea pig? Remy?"

Remy groaned. "I can't be the guinea pig," he said. "I have to pay attention. John will have to do it."

John grinned, "I don't mind," he said. "This could be a defining moment in the history of robotics."

Jane smiled. "I don't think it's going to be that historical. But I guess you could be known as the first person who was almost scanned."

"Sounds good to me," laughed John. "I'll take fame any way I can get it."

"Okay, John," said Jane, "since you're so ready to be famous, why don't you come over here?"

John walked over to the machine, where Jane was standing.

I'm almost afraid to touch anything," said Jane, hesitantly. "I feel like I'm going to break it."

John smiled at her. "How can you say that?" he asked. "Don't you know the computer credo?!"

"Oh no!" said Jane, starting to laugh. "How could I forget that?"

John cleared his throat, and then, in a deep voice said, "There is nothing that you can do that will irreversibly damage a computer!" He paused dramatically, and then said, "Except....."

"The Killer Poke!" finished Jane, as she poked John in the ribs.

The two began laughing uncontrollably.

Jane looked at John curiously as she was laughing. "Did you notice it?" she asked, through her giggles. "It's supposed to be a safeguard for the machine."

"Of course," laughed John, as he poked Jane in the ribs again. "How could I miss it? It was very clever of you! I know you've always wanted to program a Killer Poke, ever since we learned about them."

"And now I've had my chance!" said Jane, aiming a particularly energetic poke at John.

"What are you two laughing about?" said Remy, clearly annoyed. "We're supposed to be working!"

"Remy!" said John. "How could you forget Professor Parsons and our first class together? Computer History 101 was where we all met!"

"I haven't forgotten," replied Remy, "but I have no idea what you're talking about."

"That's because you were always too hungover to pay attention in class!" said Jane. "Plus, I don't think you ever studied for a test. You just cheated off John and me!"

"I never cheated," said Remy. "I just found it more efficient not to duplicate the work of others …so I borrowed a few of your answers. Now, can we get back to work? At this rate we're never going to get anything done!"

"Sure," said Jane, with a giggle, as she poked John in the ribs again. "Whatever you want."

***

About an hour later, Jane had finished her instructional session on how to use the machine, including a simulated scan of John.

"Alright…that's everything…did you both get all of that?" she asked, as she ended the shared user interface session in her Brain Band. "I can review anything that wasn't clear."

"I got it," said John. "It's really not that hard."

"I think I have everything," said Remy, slowly. "But maybe you could go over the process of initiating a scan one more time. You kind of lost me there."

116

"Sure," said Jane. "That's one of the easiest parts."

Jane repositioned John in the scanning bed. The restraints automatically adjusted around his body, holding him in place.

"Once you have your subject placed on the scanning bed," she said, "you use your Brain Band to start the initiation sequence. It's always a good idea to recheck all of the settings, but the machine has safeguards built in. It won't start scanning unless it's safe."

"That's good to know," said John, "since I'm the one strapped into it."

"Don't worry," said Jane. "We're nowhere near scanning a person yet. We still have lots of testing to do."

"After you initiate the scanning process," continued Jane, "you come over to the machine and activate it using this control panel."

Remy was following close behind Jane. "This one here?" he asked, pointing to the panel on the machine that Jane had just activated.

"Right," said Jane, "this is the main control panel. As I demonstrated before, this is the only portion of the machine that is not interfaced with our Brain Bands. It ensures that the operator is in the same room with the machine before the scan can be initiated. When you're ready to scan, you enter the security sequence to get the machine ready. The next part is where you'd be stuck without me. In order to start the scan, I have to swipe my hand over the biometric reader. This compares my palm and fingerprint information to the data stored on the machine. The initiate button only appears if there is a match."

"Can I see how that works?" asked Remy curiously.

"Uh, sure," said Jane. "I guess. But it's not going to show you much. Once I swipe my hand, the machine will switch into an active mode and allow me to press the initiate button. If someone else swiped their hand, the machine would shut down and a scan wouldn't be possible."

Jane swept her hand along a section of the control panel and the machine made a series of whirring noises. After a moment, an initiate button appeared on the screen.

"If we were actually going to do a scan," said Jane, "I'd press this button and the scanning sequence would start. Otherwise, if you'd made it to this point and then decided you weren't ready to scan, you would press cancel to shut down the machine's scanning process."

"Like this?" said Remy.

Jane was expecting Remy to press CANCEL, but instead, he pushed her hand roughly out of the way, and pressed INITIATE. The machine came to life with a soft hum.

"What have you done?" said Jane, in horror. "It's not ready yet! John....."

She trailed off as she looked over at John. The machine had begun the scanning process, and he was unable to speak or move.

"Get out of my way!" said Jane, frantically. "There's an abort button. I can still stop the scan if I do it now!"

But Remy wouldn't budge. He was standing directly in front of the control panel, blocking Jane's access. In a few moments, it was too late to stop the machine.

"This could kill him, Remy!" said Jane. "What is wrong with you? I told you the machine wasn't ready yet!"

Remy had stopped listening to Jane. He was mesmerized by the scanning process. He kept switching his focus between John and the stream of information from John's neural scan being displayed in his visual field.

"It's incredible," he said, in awe. "It's working...it's

really working!"

Jane couldn't believe what was happening. She had assumed that the machine would be thoroughly tested before it was used on a living being. And now, John was being scanned and there was nothing she could do about it.

"How long will it take?" asked Remy, still mesmerized by the process.

"About 10 minutes," said Jane, anxiously. She wanted to scream at Remy, but at the moment, she was more concerned about John. If anything happened to him, she would never be able to forgive herself.

How could she have been so stupid?

After a few more minutes, the sounds that the machine was making slowed and then stopped. John, who had been motionless the entire time, suddenly stirred in the restraints.

"Ugh," he said. "I have a headache….what happened?"

"You're alive!" said Jane, in relief.

"Of course I'm alive," said John. "I've just been lying here pointlessly for the last few minutes."

John saw the concern on Jane's face and then looked over at Remy, who was gazing at the machine triumphantly.

"You just scanned me, didn't you?" he asked.

"I think you should sit down," said Jane, as she undid the straps and led John to a chair. "We need to make sure there isn't any damage."

John looked over at Remy and for a moment it seemed as if he was going to say something unpleasant. But, before he could do so, his attention was diverted.

"Is that me?" he asked, looking in wonder at the all of the data that was scrolling rapidly before him.

"Yes," said Remy, in awe. "It's amazing!"

Remy came over and stood behind Jane. "No harm,

no foul," he said. "John's fine, the machine works, and we don't have to do lots of silly tests. Testing is a big waste of time."

Jane looked at Remy. She could hardly contain her anger.

"You just tested the machine on your best friend!" she snapped.

"Inventors always test their inventions on themselves," said Remy, flippantly. "It's how science progresses."

"Then why weren't you in there getting scanned?" asked Jane, sarcastically.

"I'm much too valuable," said Remy. "Besides, my incredible brain probably would've broken the machine."

Jane shook her head in frustration. It didn't matter what she said. It wouldn't have any impact on Remy.

John had been silent for the last few moments, staring fixedly at his own data.

"I'd like to get my algorithm working on this data," said John, excitedly. "I'd thought we'd have to test it on fake data, but now we have something real for it to chew on!"

"See," said Remy, self righteously, "I was just helping John get some data for his algorithm."

Jane glared at him and then looked over at John, still concerned.

"Are you sure you're feeling okay?" she asked. "Don't you think you want to lie down for a little while? We don't know what the side effects might be..."

John smiled at Jane and patted her hand reassuringly. "I'm fine," he said. "In fact, I've never felt better! I think that scanning machine did something to me. I feel like I could work all day!"

Jane tried to smile, but she was still worried. How could she have let this happen?

Jane turned to Remy, her face flushed red with

anger. Normally she didn't get angry. But this was different.

"So you got what you wanted Remy," she said. "But this isn't how it's going to end."

"Huh?" said Remy. He was staring in satisfaction at the new stream of information, watching John's algorithm begin to work on the data.

"I'm putting a stop to all of this. It's obvious you can't be trusted. So this is it. We're done using the machine," Jane said sharply, trying to keep from shouting.

"What!" said Remy, shocked. "We just got it working! We can't stop now!"

"We got it working at the possible price of your friend's life!" Jane said, her voice shaking with emotion. "How can I let you use the machine if you're willing to take such risks?"

Remy shrugged his shoulders and looked at Jane angrily. "But the machine didn't hurt John," he retorted. "See," he said, pointing to his friend, "he's fine!"

"You just don't get it," shouted Jane. "How can you be so blind and stupid?"

"Me! Stupid!" said Remy. "What about you? If we left science up to you nothing would ever happen. You're such a prissy goody two shoes!"

"Whoa," said John, alarmed at the tone the conversation was taking. "Maybe it's time we stopped for the day."

"I want to stop forever!" said Jane.

"You see what I'm dealing with?" said Remy to John. "She's impossible!"

John stood between his two friends. "I think we all need to take a day off," he said. "We've been working much too hard. Let's take tomorrow to cool down and think about things. And, at the end of the day, we'll talk about how we want to proceed."

Jane glared at Remy. She didn't want to cool down

and she didn't want to proceed, at least not with Remy. But part of her knew that John was right. She was exhausted and she needed rest. Maybe a day off would be a good idea.

"Fine!" said Jane, trying to keep her voice calm as she stalked out of the lab. "But don't expect me to change my mind!"

00010001

PROFESSOR CHATHAM

"You're a sight for sore eyes," smiled Professor Chatham.

Jane was connected to the lab at Malvern and had just gotten through to Professor Chatham. It was very late at night, and she hadn't been sure that he would still be at work. Luckily she'd been able to catch him before he left. She needed to talk to someone after what had happened in the lab that day.

"It's good to see you too," said Jane.

"Before I forget," said Professor Chatham, "Will said to say hi. He dropped by my office this afternoon and was asking about you."

Jane felt her face turning red. She was surprised at her own reaction. What was wrong with her? Will was nothing, just a friend. "Oh," said Jane, shortly.

"Do you want me to tell him anything?" asked Professor Chatham, with a slight smile.

Jane felt even more embarrassed. It was obvious that Professor Chatham noticed her discomfort.

"Uh," said Jane. "No…yes…no…um…just tell him I said hi too."

"Of course," he smiled, "I'll be sure to let him know.

Jane nodded, hoping he would change the subject.

"So I see you're still in one piece," he continued, "that's a good sign."

Jane frowned, her thoughts brought back to the events of the day. "Barely," she said. "Today wasn't a good day. Remy used my machine to scan John"

Professor Chatham looked at Jane in surprise. Jane had been giving him regular progress reports on her research, so he was aware that the machine existed. He also knew that it wasn't ready for use and hadn't been tested.

"Is he okay?" he asked, in concern.

"So far he seems fine," said Jane, her voice betraying her emotion. "But it could have killed him! I can't believe Remy would do something like this!"

"You can't?" asked Professor Chatham, gently.

Jane sighed. "I guess I should have known better, it's Remy after all. But John is supposed to be his best friend!"

"I don't think Remy understands the meaning of friendship," replied Professor Chatham.

Jane shook her head angrily. "He doesn't understand the meaning of anything!"

"So what are you going to do now?" asked Professor Chatham.

"I don't know," said Jane, "I don't want to have anything to do with Remy. I told him today that I was done with him and the machine!"

"Do you think that's the best course of action?" asked the professor.

"I can't work with someone like Remy...it always ends in disaster!" said Jane.

"You underestimate yourself Jane," said Professor Chatham. "Remy might be strong, but you're stronger."

Jane was silent for a few moments. "You think I should keep going?" she asked, finally.

"You have an opportunity to complete your work... work that would take decades if you didn't have the resources of Remy's lab," he said. "Remy doesn't have to be the one that controls the outcome of everything. You can be that person. You just have to start thinking the way he does. Once you do that, you'll be able to stay ahead of him."

"Maybe," said Jane, reluctantly. "I'd have to think about it."

"And here's something else to think about," said Professor Chatham, "what are you going to do when the machine is tested and it does work?"

"What do you mean?" asked Jane.

"Your machine is going to work," he continued. "You're going to be faced with a lot of decisions when that happens. Who's going to be in control of this technology when it's out in the world?"

Jane faltered, unsure of how to respond. "I hadn't really thought that far ahead."

"I thought that might be your reaction," said Professor Chatham.

"I think part of me is a little afraid that it will work," said Jane, softly.

"Of course," said Professor Chatham. "New technology is always scary. But I know you Jane. When the time comes to make an ethical decision, I know you'll make the right choice. You always have and you always will."

"But when I asked you about what you were going to do," continued Professor Chatham, "I wasn't just referring to the machine. You're the inventor of an earth shattering new piece of technology. You're going to be famous. Is Malvern University really where you're going to want to be?"

Jane didn't know what to say. She had always assumed her place would be at Malvern University. It was all she knew.

"Do you think that I'm going to leave Malvern so I can work for RJ Robotics?" asked Jane.

"I didn't say that," said Professor Chatham. "But I would like you to think about your future too. There's always a place for you at Malvern, you know that. But maybe it's time for you to move on. The world is a much bigger place than just a tiny little lab in a tiny little university."

Jane nodded slowly. She hadn't realized that completing her research and building her machine would create so many new problems. Once the machine was built, everything would be perfect...or at least that's what she'd always assumed. But now, she didn't know what to think.

00010010

DAY OFF

The next morning at breakfast, the atmosphere was still tense. Jane was very tired. She hadn't slept well, and her few short snatches of sleep had been haunted by vivid nightmares. Her conversation with Professor Chatham had helped her feel a little better, but she was still upset at Remy. She tried to avoid looking at him, but, from the corner of her eye, she could see his smug, self-satisfied face, which only increased her anger.

"So what are you going to do with your day off?" Remy asked John.

"A day off!" said John. "I haven't had one of those in a long time. I need to catch up on my journal reading. They build up so fast and I don't want to get behind. After that, I thought I might reprogram some of the new Brain Bands we've been working on…"

Ashley glared at John and then poked him roughly in the arm.

"That's not a day off, Johnny!" she said, in annoyance. "Plus, have you forgotten that we're supposed to meet with the caterers this afternoon? We have at least two or three hours of taste testing to do."

John sighed and tried to look pleased. "Sorry dear," he said. "I did forget, but that sounds much better than reading journals and programming."

Ashley smiled happily. "Good!" she said. "You won't spend your day being a total dork, for a change! Also, after we finish with the caterers, the wedding planner wants us to start looking at fabric colors for the napkins at the reception. It's very important we pick just the right color. The wrong color could ruin the entire evening!"

John nodded solemnly, trying hard to look as if he understood the importance of napkin colors.

Jane looked away from John. She thought she might laugh if she caught his eye, and that would only make matters worse. Poor John...he was in for a day of suffering.

"You can join us if you'd like, Jane," said Ashley, graciously. "You wouldn't get a say in any of the decisions, but it might be nice for you. Unless it would make you feel depressed....you know, since you're probably never going to find someone to marry...."

Jane tried not to let the horror she felt show in her face. A day spent wedding planning with Ashley would be worse than torture!

"Thanks so much," said Jane. "I'd love to, but I think I need to get a little rest."

"Suit yourself," said Ashley, "but you're definitely going to miss a day of fun."

"What are you going to do today, Jane?" asked Remy, politely.

Jane didn't look at him as she answered. She still didn't want to talk to him, but she had to try to be civil.

"I'm not sure..." she began, before Remy interrupted her.

"I'm going into town today and you're welcome to come with me," said Remy. "Otherwise, you haven't had much time to admire my beautiful island. You should walk around and check out the place. It's pretty nice, if I do say so myself."

Jane felt a bit surprised. Normally Remy didn't show any concern or interest in anyone but himself. What was going on this morning? He was almost being nice! Perhaps he was trying to make up for yesterday.

128

"That actually sounds good to me," said Jane. "I could use some fresh air."

"Great," said Remy. "Then it's decided. We all have plans for the day!"

--

Jane took a deep breath as she walked away from the mansion. According to Remy, after the formal gardens that bordered the house, there were miles of trails that she could spend the day exploring. It was a beautiful summer day, warm but not too hot, perfect weather for a long walk.

The walk would do her good after so many days cooped up in the lab. Plus, she needed time to think. The events of the previous day had upset her deeply.

Jane walked through the gardens that surrounded Remy's mansion, marveling at their beauty. She knew that Remy wasn't an expert on flowers and gardening, but he certainly knew how to hire people who were. The grounds were incredible.

"Only the best for Remy," muttered Jane.

She sighed as she thought about Remy. He was so difficult for her to understand. He wasn't trustworthy, but at the same time, there was something about him that made her want to believe in him. "The Remy spell…," she said to herself, musingly.

As she had learned yesterday, Remy plus her machine was not a good combination. Jane's anger welled up again as she thought about how Remy had tricked her and scanned John. How could he have done such a thing? And how could she have allowed it to happen?

As Jane continued walking away from the mansion, she felt a sudden shift in her feelings. She stopped for a moment, deep in thought.

"I'm not mad at Remy," she said to herself, slowly. "I'm mad at myself."

As Professor Chatham had pointed out the previous day, it wasn't surprising that Remy had scanned John. In fact, Jane had been expecting him to do something underhanded. She knew Remy too well. He was always going to lie, cheat, or steal to get his own way.

"But I let him...again," said Jane, in frustration.

Jane thought back to the day when Remy had betrayed her in college. She had tried to stand up to him then, but it had been much too late. Part of her felt that she was to blame for what had happened. If she had only been able to stand up to Remy from the beginning of their relationship, maybe things would have been different. But she had never been able to. And, because of that, Remy didn't treat her with respect. He took advantage of her any chance he got.

And her solution to dealing with Remy was always the same...running away. Professor Chatham had alluded to that in their conversation.

"Running away doesn't solve anything," sighed Jane. "It just makes things worse."

Jane thought more about what Professor Chatham had said to her. Did he really think that she was stronger than Remy? And what had he meant when he'd said to start thinking like Remy? In her past interactions with Remy, Jane had always acted as if he was guided by the same values as she was. But he clearly wasn't. In fact, Remy thought ethics and honesty were a waste of time.

"But that's the problem," said Jane, as realization dawned on her. "Remy doesn't think like me. That's why he always wins." Jane was lost in thought for a few moments. "Maybe I am stronger than Remy," she said, softly. "I've just never given myself a chance."

Jane walked for a few moments, turning everything over in her mind. "This time I'm not going to run away," she said, finally.

She could outsmart Remy and still stay true to herself. She just had to play the game in a different way.

***

Jane had reached the crest of a hill and was sitting on large rock at the edge of the woods. She could see glimpses of the water through the trees. The spot was beautiful and very peaceful, a perfect place to gather her thoughts before heading back to the mansion.

Her anger against Remy had subsided and she was ready to face him again.

But there was more that she had to think about before she started walking back. The points that Professor Chatham had brought up were still unresolved. What was she going to do about the machine? And what about her own future?

In the past, all she had ever thought about was the good she could do with her research. Once her machine was built and working, she would be able to help millions of sick and suffering people….at least that was her dream. But that's what it had always been….a dream! She had always assumed her work would take so long that she wouldn't be able to finish it during her lifetime. But now, here she was, with a working machine and brain scans from Bunnykins and John. So why wasn't she more excited?

"Remy," muttered Jane to herself, "and people like him!"

Remy was so obsessed with power and money. And he wasn't the only one. Corporations only existed to make money. And she was certain that they would find a way to turn her machine into a marketable product, just as Remy wanted to do. Jane didn't want her machine to be used to produce overpriced gadgets that companies could sell. She wanted it to be used for more noble purposes, helping those in need and healing those who were suffering.

And then there was the question of her own future. Professor Chatham had made a good point. Once the machine was out in the world, her life would be completely different. Jane had never wanted fame or fortune, but it was going to be hard to avoid.

"I like my life the way it is," said Jane. "Why does it have to change?"

***

About an hour later, Jane was heading back towards the mansion. She'd had a beautiful, restful day walking around the island. She still hadn't resolved everything in her mind, but she knew that she was ready to talk to Remy.

Jane had just reached the rose garden, when she realized that she wasn't alone.

One of the gardeners was also outside, methodically pruning the rose bushes.

Jane walked over to the gardener, admiring the roses as she went. She didn't normally like roses, but these were absolutely beautiful, and they smelled wonderful too.

"Hi," said Jane, waving to the gardener as she walked up next to him.

The man paused for a moment in his work and then turned slowly towards her. He looked at her blankly for a moment, and then said, in a monotone voice, "Helllo, Jane."

Jane tried not to be put off by the man's strange manner. It seemed that all of Remy's staff knew her name and weren't very good at small talk.

"These roses are lovely!" said Jane, enthusiastically. "What's the old saying? A rose by any other name wouldn't smell as sweet? I think these roses would be beautiful even if they were called cabbages," she joked.

The man looked at her blankly for a few moments. Finally, he made a sound that resembled a laugh.

Jane tried not to let the aversion she felt show on her face. This man was creepy!

Jane started to back away from the man slowly. But, before she could get very far, he put his hand on her arm and gripped it strongly.

The man raised his pruning shears above his head and, for a moment, Jane thought that he was going to attack her.

Then, he laughed and waved the shears, as if in a parting gesture. "Have a good day, Jane," he said.

Jane pulled her arm free and walked away from the man quickly. She almost stumbled in her haste to get away, but was able to right herself in time. She wanted to run, but she tried to act as normal as possible. After a few minutes of quick walking, Jane glanced around. The gardener was back at work. Jane sighed in relief. At least he wasn't following her.

"Am I being paranoid?" Jane asked herself. The man looked totally normal now, just another staff person hard at work.

But he wasn't normal! In fact, all of Remy's staff made her feel uncomfortable.

"Leave it to Remy," said Jane, ruefully. "He probably gets a kick from creeping out his guests."

00010011

MAN IN THE NIGHT

When Jane got back to the mansion, she was surprised to find an empty house.

John and Remy had been called into town for an unexpected meeting with one of their investors that evening. They weren't going to return until the next day. And Ashley was at the strip club and wasn't coming back until very late that night.

She was alone.

"A night of peace and quiet," said Jane to herself. "Finally!"

***

Jane woke up with a start. It was the middle of the night and she'd just had another nightmare. She couldn't remember the details, but her heart was pounding when she woke up and she was covered in sweat. It couldn't have been good.

"I'm not going to get much sleep tonight," sighed Jane.

Jane turned on the lights and got out of bed.

"Maybe some tea and a walk will do me good," she said, as she pulled on a robe and pushed her feet into her slippers.

After several days staying at the huge mansion, Jane still found it a confusing maze, but she knew how to get to a few places, including the kitchen.

Or at least she thought she did.

After walking down two long hallways and

descending a flight of stairs, Jane had to admit to herself that she was lost. In her mind, the kitchen should be in front of her, but, instead, she was at the entrance to a hallway that she had never seen before.

Jane wondered if she should try to retrace her steps and get back to her room. She peered down the dimly lit hallway, trying to see if she could make out anything familiar.

As she looked, Jane breathed a sigh of relief. There, at the end of the hallway, was one of the household staff. He'd be able to direct her to the kitchen and then back to her room.

Jane proceeded rapidly down the hallway, happy that she was no longer alone in the house. However, as she got closer to the man, her steps slowed.

"What is he doing?" she asked herself, as she stood watching him.

The man was at the very end of the hallway, in front of a heavily curtained window and a small decorative table. He kept walking towards the wall, bumping into it, and then backing up and doing the same thing, over and over again. As he did so, he mumbled the same phrase.

"Go back to the lab, go back to the lab," he said, in a low, quaking voice.

Jane was appalled. What was wrong with him?

Jane walked towards the man slowly. She didn't want to startle him. She reached out and touched his arm gently.

"Excuse me sir," she said softly. "Is there something wrong?"

The man didn't even look at her. It was if he wasn't aware of her presence.

Jane touched his arm again and said loudly, "Sir, is there something I can help you with?"

Just as before, the man didn't respond. Instead, he kept walking into the wall and mumbling to himself. Jane watched him for a moment. There was something about the man that frightened her, something almost inhuman.

Despite her fears, Jane knew that she had to get the man some help. He was clearly suffering from some horrible ailment.

Just then, Jane heard the sound of someone walking briskly down the hallway. Hopefully whoever it was would be able to get help.

She was about to call out, when she felt someone grab her from behind. Before she could make a sound, a hand covered her mouth and she was pulled roughly backwards into a dark room.

***

Jane struggled to face her attacker. She wrenched herself free and turned around quickly, before she could be grabbed again. It took a moment for her eyes to adjust to the darkness. She was standing in a small room off the hallway, and there, before her, was the last person she had expected to see that evening.

"Will!" she said, shocked. "What are you doing here? And why on earth did you grab me like that?"

Will motioned to her to be quiet. "I'll explain later," he said. "But we have to be quiet. There's someone coming."

"But," protested Jane, "we have to get that man help…"

"Shhh," interrupted Will. "If we're caught here it's not going to be good."

Jane was silenced by Will's serious tone. What was he talking about? Nothing was making any sense.

Will opened the door a tiny crack and peered out. Jane stood behind him, looking over his shoulder.

She could hear someone coming down the hallway. The person was talking loudly.

"I know, Remy! That's why I'm trying to find him before anyone else does. He's supposed to be somewhere in this hallway."

Jane almost gasped aloud. It was Ashley, talking loudly to someone using her Brain Band.

"Yes . . . Of course I have it with me. Yeah . . . I know that! I can see his navigation identifier on the internal map . . . But I don't see HIM! Well, if you were here and not out partying tonight, maybe this wouldn't have happened," Ashley snapped.

"Oh, wait a sec," she continued. "I see him. He's at the end of the hallway."

"Huh?" she said. "Yes, I know what to do. I've done it before!"

Ashley paused for a moment, and then said, "Yeah, I got it. I'll see you tomorrow. Love ya, brother!"

Ashley tromped down to the end of the hallway, her high heels clicking sharply on the hard wood floor.

When she reached the man, she stopped and looked at him. Then she started laughing loudly.

"So that's where you've been all evening!" she said. "Remy said you were malfunctioning. It looks like he was right."

Ashley poked and prodded the man a few times, but with no effect. He continued to run into the wall, muttering to himself all the time.

"This is too funny," she snorted, watching the man with obvious amusement. "But it's late, and I've had enough fun for one night."

As Will and Jane watched, Ashley slipped off her Brain Band and pulled another one from her pocket. This one was different, much smaller and slimmer. Ashley put this Brain Band on and looked at the man. Immediately, he stopped and turned all of his attention towards her.

"Follow me," she said, with a giggle. "We're off to the scrap heap!"

Ashley turned sharply on her heel and began

marching down the hallway. The man, without another sound, followed after her.

After a few minutes, Will breathed out a long sigh. "It's worse than I thought," he muttered, half to himself.

"What are you talking about?" said Jane. You owe me an explanation! Why are you here and what's going on?"

Will looked up absently. "Of course," he said, trying to bring his attention back to Jane. "But first, let's get back to your room. We can talk there."

"That might be a problem," said Jane, nervously. "The only reason I'm here is because I got lost trying to find the kitchen."

"Don't worry," said Will, taking Jane by the arm and leading her out of the room. "I know where we're going."

00010100

WILL

A few moments later, Jane and Will were back in her room.

"Quite a place you've got," said Will, looking around at the gaudily decorated space. "It looks like a psychedelic safari in here."

"It's the leopard room," sighed Jane, as she locked the door behind them. "Ashely thought I'd like it."

Will nodded. "I should I have known," he said. "I can see Ashley all over this space. How do you sleep in here?"

"I don't," said Jane ruefully. "But that's not important right now. What I want to know is how you know your way around the house?"

"I spent a lot of time here in my younger days," replied Will. "Back when Remy and I were friends…or at least what Remy considers a friend. His definition leaves a bit to be desired."

Jane nodded. "I know what you mean."

She paused for a moment, and then said, "I'd offer you some snacks, but I don't have anything here. That's why I was going to the kitchen…to get something to eat."

Will smiled and reached for his bag. "I have anything you could possibly want," he said.

He picked up the bag and dumped it out on the bed. Jane gazed in amazement at the huge pile of snack food and candy.

"Why do you have all of this stuff?" she asked.

"I was doing a stakeout," said Will. "I didn't know how long I was going to be sneaking around the house. I didn't want to get hungry."

"Here," he continued, grabbing some snacks from the pile. "From me to you."

Jane took the offered snack and then wrinkled her nose as she looked at it more closely. "Ugh, beef jerky!" she said. "Do you have anything else? You know I'm a vegetarian."

"I know," said Will, "so am I. It's vegan beef jerky. It's actually pretty good," he added, as he bit into a piece.

Jane looked at Will in surprise. "I didn't know you were a vegetarian too!"

"There's a lot you don't know about me," he replied. "Anyway, try it," he added encouragingly. "You'll love it!"

Jane looked at the beef jerky skeptically, and then opened the package and took a bite. "Not bad," she said, with a smile. "I haven't had beef jerky in years."

"It's good stakeout food," said Will, returning Jane's smile.

"Why were you doing a stakeout in the first place?" demanded Jane, her thoughts returning to the events in the hallway. "How did you even get here?"

"I have a friend with a boat," said Will, with a slight smile. "One of the regulars at the bar...he owed me a favor."

"Why doesn't that surprise me!" said Jane. "But what are you doing here?"

"It's hard to wrap my head around everything," said Will, with a sigh. "But I'll do my best to explain."

"Do you remember I mentioned that Remy had been hanging out at the soup kitchen where I volunteer?" asked Will.

Jane nodded her head. "Yes," she said. "You said he didn't come to help out, but he was just showing up

142

every so often."

"Right," said Will. "Well, a little while ago I noticed that some of our regulars weren't coming anymore. I didn't think too much of it at first. Most of the people who come to the soup kitchen are transient. They don't have homes or families or stable lives. For the most part, no one notices if they disappear."

"What does all this have to do with what we saw tonight?" asked Jane.

"A few weeks ago," continued Will, "one of our most loyal customers, Matthew Armstrong, just stopped coming. Like I said before, it normally isn't a big deal when people don't show up. But this particular person is rich and famous….he's a fixture of the community. And he just disappeared without a trace!"

Jane looked at Will in surprise. "I think I saw something on the news about that," she said. "Nobody knows what happened to him. But why was he going to the soup kitchen?"

"He has a reputation for being extremely thrifty," said Will. "For him, it was a way to save money on food."

Jane nodded thoughtfully. "The whole story is crazy," she said, "but I still don't see how Remy fits in."

"After Matthew disappeared," said Will, "I started thinking about when the disappearances began. It was right around the time that Remy started coming to the soup kitchen."

Jane gasped. "Do you think Remy has something to do with them?" she asked.

"I don't know," said Will slowly. "But I have a bad feeling. The first few times he came, he asked me all sorts of weird questions about the people who came to the soup kitchen. I thought he was just curious, but now, I don't know."

Will paused for a moment and then said, "I didn't know what to do. How could I go to the police and accuse Remy of being involved with homeless people disappearing? I don't have any proof besides a bad feeling! The only thing I could think of doing was to come here and take a look around."

Will paused for a moment, and then said, "Plus, I was worried about you."

"Me?" said Jane in surprise. "What do I have to do with anything?"

"I've been getting updates about you from my uncle," said Will, his face reddening slightly. "I thought you might need some help, especially if Remy is up to something bad."

Jane tried not to look at Will. She could feel herself blushing.

"Oh," she said, not sure what else to say. She was actually extremely happy to see Will, but she didn't know why. Perhaps all of the difficulties with Remy were making her overly anxious.

"The man in the hallway," said Jane, attempting to change the subject, "was he Matthew Armstrong?"

Will shook his head. "No," he answered grimly. "But he was one of our regulars. Or at least, what's left of him."

Jane nodded, trying to comprehend everything Will had just told her. But her head was in a whirl. She could hardly believe everything she had seen and heard that evening! There was too much going on for her to make sense of it all. She felt as if she had all of the pieces of the puzzle, but, she still didn't know how to fit them together. Remy and John and RJ Robotics, her machine and John's scanning algorithms, the man in the hallway... somehow everything was connected, she just didn't know how.

"We'll have to talk to Remy tomorrow and see what he's gotten into this time," she sighed. "I'm sure he already knows you're here. Computers monitor everything on the island."

"I figured as much," replied Will. "Remy always seems to be a few steps ahead. But we'll be ready for him tomorrow. And maybe it won't be as bad as we think...who knows, there might be an innocent explanation for everything."

Jane nodded and tried to push aside her forebodings. Maybe Will was right. Maybe there was an innocent explanation. She took a deep breath, trying to calm her nerves. She needed to get a good night's sleep if she was going to face Remy in the morning.

"We'll know soon enough," said Jane, hoping her voice didn't betray the dread that she felt.

00010101

ROMANCE

"I think it's about time we went to bed," said Jane, looking at the clock on her bedside table.

"I hope I can sleep," said Will, "I have a really bad stomachache."

"I'm not surprised," replied Jane. "You ate almost all of the junk that you brought with you."

Will looked regretfully at the few remaining snacks that were on the bed. "I guess I shouldn't have eaten so much," he said. "But it's not like I didn't have help!"

"I was stress eating," said Jane defensively. "It was a very difficult evening. Plus, you definitely ate most of them!"

Will smiled and pushed the remaining snacks from the bed into his bag.

"Well, what do you say," he said, patting the bed. "It's probably time we hit the hay."

Jane looked at him in surprise. "It's time I hit the hay, you mean," she said firmly. "You're sleeping on the floor with Bunnykins!"

Will looked hurt. "What do you think of me?" he asked. "I'd be the perfect gentleman! We'd each have our own sides of the bed and I wouldn't come near you. I promise!"

Jane looked at him skeptically. "You've definitely changed, but I still don't trust you enough to let you have half the bed. So it's either the floor….or nothing."

Will sighed in resignation. "Fine," he said, "but at

least give me a few extra pillows and blankets. I'm too old to be sleeping on the floor."

Jane threw a few pillows at him. Will grabbed the pillows and began constructing a makeshift bed on the floor.

"You won't trust me to sleep next to you, but you're okay with me next to your beloved rabbit," he grumbled.

Jane looked from Will to Bunnykins. "That's a good point," she said.

Will smiled triumphantly and began gathering up his pillows to bring back into the bed. But, before he could make much progress, Jane reached down and gently picked up Bunnykins.

"Bunnykins, you're sleeping in the bed with me tonight," she said.

Will groaned and then smiled at Jane. "I see where I stand in the scheme of things," he said. "I'm not even as important as your pet rabbit."

Jane laughed and said, "Of course not, no one's as important as Bunnkyins."

***

A few moments later, Jane was drifting off to sleep, when she was startled by a voice coming from the floor.

"Jane, can you sleep?"

Jane reluctantly opened her eyes. She had almost forgotten that Will was in the room with her.

"I could if you'd stop talking," she said.

"Sorry," said Will, "but I'm having trouble sleeping. Maybe if I was in the bed...." he began.

"No," said Jane firmly. "That's not going to work!"

"It was worth a try," said Will, with a laugh. "I thought you might take pity on me down here."

"No," said Jane. "I'm pretty sure you'll survive one night sleeping on the floor."

"If I don't," said Will, "you'll have it on your conscience forever."

Jane laughed. "I'll try to be okay with that," she said.

Will sighed and then said, more seriously, "I just keep thinking about Remy. I don't know how I keep getting mixed up with him."

"I understand," replied Jane. "I thought I was done with Remy too."

"He has a way of sucking people in," said Will. "There's something about him. It's like he puts a spell on you that can't be broken."

Jane was silent for a moment, and then said, "Will, what was it that happened between you and Remy? Your uncle never really told me the whole story."

Will didn't answer for a few minutes and Jane began to wonder if he'd fallen asleep.

Finally, he said, "It's not a part of my life that I'm very proud of. I wasn't a good kid growing up."

"You knew Remy before you moved in with your uncle?" asked Jane.

"I met him when I was a senior in high school," said Will. "I was still living with my mother then. But she had her own problems and didn't really care what I was doing. I basically raised myself….kind of like Remy, I guess. No one ever looked after him either."

"Remy told me his parents died when he and Ashley were little kids," said Jane, thoughtfully. "Wasn't there an uncle or some other family member who stepped in to take care of them?"

"You could say that," said Will, with a short laugh. "There were a few family members who tried to supervise Remy and Ashely, but most of them gave up and passed them on to the next relative. They were wild. No one could keep them under control."

"Not much has changed," said Jane.

"Yeah," said Will, "except I think they were even worse as kids, if you can believe that. Anyway, Remy liked to hang around the public school. He was at some ritzy private school, but he liked to spend time in the city. Looking for excitement, I guess...or trouble, or both."

"So you were friends with him?" asked Jane.

"If you could call it friends," replied Will. "I was into some bad things back then and so was Remy. I'm sure I would have gotten in trouble anyway, but Remy made everything much worse. At first, I thought he was fun and cool. I wanted to be like him. We got into all sorts of trouble together, but Remy always seemed to find a way out of it. Until the night when I got arrested, and he didn't. Remy was much smarter than me, and much more devious."

"What happened?" asked Jane, softly.

"We were out partying with a bunch of his prep school friends, drinking, doing all sorts of things we shouldn't have been doing. Remy and I decided we were going to go for a drive. He said he'd brought his new car with him that night and he wanted to try it out with me. It was incredible! The most expensive car I'd ever seen in my life. I was drunk, but Remy said he'd drive. I just went along with him. I don't remember the crash, but I do remember waking up in the driver's seat by myself with the police looking down on me."

"Remy was gone?" asked Jane.

"Yup," said Will, ruefully. "He'd cleared out on his best pal Will, to let him take the rap for drunk driving and stealing a car."

"Oh my gosh," said Jane, shocked. "The car wasn't his?"

"No," said Will. "What's funny is that he had an even nicer car. I mean, he's super rich...he could have any car he wanted. But he wanted to experience the thrill of stealing a car. Somehow he figured out a way to hack the car's computer and get the engine started. But he wasn't going to get in trouble. Not the untouchable Remy. So he left me to take the blame."

"Did you go to jail?" asked Jane. "Drunk driving and stealing a car... that's pretty serious."

"Well, the police certainly knew that I wasn't smart enough to hack the car's computer, but I wouldn't tell them who did it. I ended up with 3 months in jail, and it would have been more if it wasn't for my uncle. Let's just say that it didn't take the whole 3 months to figure out that my life needed a new direction. When I got out, my uncle took me in and helped me with the court and the judge. I ended up with a lot of community service time, but that was the end of my criminal career. If it wasn't for him, I don't know what would have happened to me."

Jane was silent for a moment. She'd never realized Will had been through so much. He wasn't the person she thought he was.

"Your uncle is pretty amazing," she said, finally. "But it sounds like you've made a lot of good changes on your own too."

"It's taken me awhile," replied Will. "When you're a bartender, it's hard not to end up drinking and partying too much. But it feels like I'm finally getting my life together. I have a plan and a direction...."

Will trailed off and then said, "And now I have Remy back in my life to screw everything up again."

Jane reached down and touched Will on the shoulder. "I feel the same way, Will," she said, gently. "But we won't let that happen again."

Will reached up and squeezed Jane's hand. "For either of us," he said. "My uncle's told me some of what Remy did to you. I'm so sorry."

Jane stiffened for a moment and almost pulled her hand away. She never talked about what happened with Remy with anyone. But suddenly, she felt as if she could talk to Will. She knew he would understand.

Jane squeezed Will's hand in return. "It was horrible,

but I survived. Your uncle helped me through it. And I learned a lot of lessons that I needed to learn. I think it helped me to grow up a little too."

"My uncle always says that bad experiences make us stronger, if we let them," said Will. "We're both stronger than we were five or ten years ago. And together, I know we're strong enough to face Remy."

"You're right," said Jane. "We won't let him win, not this time."

00010110

TRUTH

"So you two finally decided to get out of bed!"

Jane and Will had just walked into the dining room. It was well after noon, and they hadn't expected anyone to be there so late. But Ashley was heaping food onto her plate from a breakfast buffet that was laid out on the table.

"Help yourselves," she said. "I'm sure you must be hungry. I don't mind sharing since I know you two vegetarians won't take any of the good stuff! More bacon for me!" Ashley cackled.

Jane was still a bit groggy after a night of very little sleep. She had been haunted by disturbing dreams of Remy using her machine. There was something Remy had kept saying in her dream that she couldn't remember. For some reason, it seemed very important. Jane had been hoping she'd have some quiet time at breakfast to think about it, but now she had Ashley to deal with.

"Will," continued Ashley, "before you sit down, could you hand me my purse? It's over there on the chair behind you. I'm running low on lipstick."

Will looked at Ashley in annoyance. "You don't seem surprised to see me," he said, as he walked across the room to retrieve the bag.

Ashley laughed as Will handed her the bag. "Of course not," she said. "Remy and I know everything that goes on in our house!"

Ashley retrieved a few tubes of lipstick from her bag and spread them out on the table.

"I can never decide what color to go with," she said gravely, as if making a crucial decision.

After a few moments of thought, she picked up one of the tubes. "Blood red," she said. "I think that's right for today!"

"So you've been watching and listening to everything we've been doing?" asked Will.

"Of course!" said Ashley, gleefully. "We see everything! It's our house, so why not?"

"Not that it matters," she continued, as she bit into a piece of bacon. "I was expecting a show last night and I was very disappointed. You could have at least slept in the same bed. That might have led to something. As it was, I stayed up late for nothing. All I got to do was listen to you two talk...boring!"

Jane looked at Ashley in disgust, but remained silent.

"Aren't you going to eat anything?" asked Ashley, who was helping herself to seconds. "There's enough food here for more than just me!"

"I'm not hungry," said Jane.

Will grabbed a plate and put a few things on it for him and Jane to share. Then he sat down at the table next to Jane.

"Do you know when John and Remy are going to be back?" asked Will.

"Anytime now," said Ashley. "John needs to be here because we're meeting with our wedding planner and a caterer today. This is our second caterer! Can you believe it? The first one was a total disaster. You should have seen the appetizers he wanted us to serve. Everything was healthy and he wanted us to have a veggie tray! Ugh! Who wants a veggie tray at a wedding? I made it very clear that I don't want that kind of food…

154

Ashley chattered on, oblivious to the fact that Jane and Will weren't listening to her.

Will put some food in front of Jane, who forced herself to eat. Dealing with Ashley always made her lose her appetite.

"Oh yeah," said Ashley. "I almost forgot. Remy wants to see both of you later today. He said to meet him in the library at 3:00. And you better not take too long talking to him. Remember, my birthday party is tonight!

"Another party?" groaned Will.

"Try to sound a little more excited," said Ashley. "My birthday parties are incredible! I thought that's why you came to the island anyway…to see me and to crash my party," she giggled flirtatiously.

Will rolled his eyes and looked away. "Not so much," he said.

"I guess I'll have to officially invite you now, since you're here. And we'll have to find something for you to wear, since it is a costume party, but that shouldn't be too hard. We have lots of extra costumes, even something for Jane here. Anyway, it's going to take everyone time to get in their costumes. And I don't want either of you to ruin my party by being late! So keep things short with Remy."

***

"Finally, the two lovebirds," said Remy, with a laugh, as Jane and Will walked into the library.

"Or maybe lovebirds is the wrong word. From what Ashley tells me you weren't too lovey last night!"

Jane glared at him and then said, "Remy, we need you to be serious. We have something important to talk to you about."

"I already know what you want to talk about!" said Remy, dismissively. "And it's making me tired!"

Remy sighed and sank down into one of the leather chairs in the middle of the room.

"You're always so serious!" he said, as he gestured for the two of them to sit down as well. "Why can't you ever be more fun?" he asked.

"Our versions of fun aren't compatible," said Jane, shortly.

"Always a party pooper," said Remy. "I was hoping Will would be a good influence on you. He used to be a lot of fun!"

"Welcome," he added, glancing over at Will. "Normally I like to invite my guests, but I wanted to talk to you anyway, so it all works out."

"We saw the man in the hallway last night!" interrupted Jane. "What's going on?"

Remy looked at Jane for a moment, and then sighed in resignation.

"I guess I should start at the beginning, since you're not going to let me have any peace until I explain everything. If we were to look at the entire field of robotics right now, what would we see? The same thing everywhere… everyone is scurrying about, trying to create the perfect humanoid robot, using the same outdated techniques that have been around for years. I was guilty of that too. But, after wasting thousands of hours, I realized that I was going about it the wrong way. Evolution has already done the work for me! I was trying to reinvent the wheel, when I already had the perfect wheel right in front of me!"

"What are you talking about?" snapped Jane, impatiently.

"You asked me to explain, so I'm explaining," said Remy. "But you have to let me do it in my own way. Anyway, as I was saying, before you so rudely interrupted…the main problem with robotics up to now has been creating a structure for the robot. You need motors and actuators and sensors and elaborate programs just to make the robot do a few pathetic tasks.

156

I realized what a waste of time all that nonsense was when I first started working on my humanoid robot. Why build what already exists? If we use people, all that work has already been done for us! We have the perfect shell for a robot. Instead of humanoid robots we have human robots. It's the perfect solution!"

Jane and Will exchanged a horrified glance. What was Remy trying to say?

"You don't mean to tell me that the man we saw last night is a robot?" said Jane, in disbelief.

"He can't be," said Will. "I recognized him. He's from the homeless shelter."

"Just another bum, like all the rest of them," said Remy, dismissively.

Jane was silent for a few moments. She had been holding onto the hope that her suspicions about Remy and the machine were unfounded. But it was clear now that Remy was deeply involved in something terrible. She needed to know the truth.

"Remy," said Jane slowly, "what are you doing to these people?"

"I'm making them better!" said Remy. "Except for that wacky musician, he was a bit of a mistake. But honestly, how was I supposed to know he was rich and famous? I mean what kind of man eats at a soup kitchen every day? All of those other men were complete wastes. I took them, brought them here, did a little tweaking, and made them useful."

"I don't understand what you're talking about," said Will. "How are you making them better? There's nothing wrong with them."

"Oh yes there is," shouted Remy harshly. "They're nothing…they're nobodies! I make them into something! I control them. I'm completely in control of everything they do!"

Jane looked at Remy in horror as realization dawned

on her. She had just remembered what she had dreamt about the previous evening. Remy, shouting the word control over and over again as he pushed people into her machine to be scanned. All of the pieces that had made no sense to her had suddenly fallen into place. She knew what Remy was doing.

"Control," she whispered to herself, her face pale.

"The control algorithm," she continued. "You used my machine to find it."

"Yes," said Remy. "I did find it... before you even got here . . .and I've been using it! It's so beautifully simple, just a little piece of code, and it gives me power over everything, the whole brain...movement, behavior, emotions! Whatever I want!"

"But that's not possible," said Jane, her voice shaking. She didn't want to believe what Remy was saying.

"Oh yes it is," said Remy, with a sharp laugh. "You've seen the results! And I don't see why you're so glum! This is the biggest breakthrough in technology since Brain Bands...and you helped make it happen!"

"Anyway," said Remy. "Before you get all self righteous on me, how about we do a demonstration? You haven't seen what these robots can do!"

Remy looked down at his watch. "It should be just about time."

As if on cue, Ashley and John entered the room, with one of Remy's household staff in tow.

"Perfect timing!" said Remy. "I was just telling Will and Jane here that we're going to have a little show."

Ashley laughed. "Wonderful!" she said. "I could use some entertainment."

John looked confused at the unexpected presence of Will. "Hey, Will," he said, uncertainly. "What are you doing here?"

"Ask Remy," said Will shortly.

"What's this all about Remy?" John asked.

"You'll see in just one minute," said Remy, as he began interfacing with his Brain Band. "I have to admit that I haven't been completely honest with you, John," he added. "But once you see this, you'll forgive me for any little white lies I had to tell you."

John walked across the room to where Will and Jane were sitting. "What's going on?" he whispered to Jane, as he took a seat on the couch next to her.

Jane could only shake her head. She couldn't find the words to explain.

"Alright," said Remy. "Watch…and be amazed at what you see!"

Ashley giggled expectantly.

"This gentleman," said Remy, gesturing towards his staff member, who was standing stiffly in the middle of the room, "will now do a few parlor tricks to entertain us."

"Bark like a dog!" said Remy.

Immediately, the man began barking in imitation of a dog.

"Stop!" said Remy imperiously. "Now stand on one foot!"

The man lifted one leg off the floor, balancing on the other.

"Now," said Remy, "I want you to…."

Before he could finish his command, Ashley shouted, "Make him dance!"

"Ah yes," said Remy. "We'll move on to a more complex behavior."

"Do a jig!" shouted Remy.

As soon as Remy had spoken, the man broke into a complicated dance, hopping and skipping about the floor.

Will, Jane, and John all watched in spellbound amazement at the man. It was a horrifying spectacle.

"Enough," said Jane, finally. "You've had your fun. Make the poor man stop."

"You spoil everything," said Remy. "It was just getting good."

Remy took off his Brain Band and the man abruptly stopped his dancing and left the room.

"What did you do to that man?" asked John, aghast at what he had just seen.

"Oh John," said Remy. "Don't tell me you don't have any idea! All of the questions I've been asking you and all of the algorithms you've come up with. That beautiful machine of Jane's just sitting in our lab unused....you can't be that stupid!"

John looked at Remy, shocked. "You don't mean to tell me...." he trailed off.

"It's the control algorithm," said Jane. "He used my machine to find it. And he's been using it to make robots out of innocent people."

"You make it sound like I'm committing some kind of crime!" protested Remy. "I'm doing good for these people! If it wasn't for me, they'd have nothing to do but live out their sorry lives as a drain on the system. Some of them even become criminals. I give them a chance to do something good for humankind, and in the process I make them better!"

John shook his head in horror, "Remy," he began. "You can't do this..."

"I already am doing it!" said Remy. "And it's going to make all of us even richer and more famous that we ever dreamed! Jane, you act like you don't care about money, but I don't believe you. Everyone wants money. And this is going to make us trillions!"

Will looked at Remy uncertainly, still finding it hard to believe everything he had seen. "I don't think I completely understand. I'm not a computer scientist like the rest of you. Are you really controlling these people's brains?"

"Bingo!" said Remy, gleefully. "That exactly what I'm doing! I find a good candidate, scan their brain, and then run the control algorithm. Once I do that, I'm the one in charge and running the show. I have a completely compliant robot! I tell them what to do and they do it!"

"And, what's even more amazing," continued Remy, "is that I can make them better. I take skills from one brain and implant them in another. Once I find the pattern for a particular set of skills, say playing a musical instrument for instance, I can give that skill to someone else. It's incredible. I can customize my robots to do whatever I want!"

"But they're still people," said Will. "You can't turn them into your puppets!"

"I get what you're saying," said Remy. "It's a new idea…it might take a while for people to get used it. But once they do, everyone will realize how amazing this is!

"But at what cost?" asked Jane, sharply.

"What do you mean?" replied Remy.

"What about the people that you're doing this to?" continued Jane. "Don't they have a say in what happens to them? I assume you didn't ask them for their consent before turning them into robots! And it's clear that your system isn't perfect. The man we saw last night didn't seem like the perfect robot. You're destroying innocent people for your own selfish ends!"

Remy sighed in frustration. "So I've run into a few glitches. It's new technology…that's bound to happen! But that's why I wanted you to come here, Jane, to help me work out a few bugs. The robots I've made so far have a short shelf life. All of that extra brain activity short circuits them eventually. They run into some kind of 'looping' program where they just keep doing the same thing over and over again. That's when it's time to get rid of them. And some of the more 'human' functions, like emotions and humor don't work that well. But I know that we can figure this out together....we're geniuses!"

"People aren't disposable," said Jane, looking at Remy in disgust. "How can you not understand that?"

"These aren't really people!" said Remy. "They're useless, until I get my hands on them! Plus, once you help me fix the machine, they'll last much longer...."

"You really think I'm going to help you?" she asked, in disbelief.

"Of course!" said Remy. "This work is going to revolutionize the entire field. Once we get going, we're going to be able to start churning out human robots by the hundreds, with a little help from Will of course. We need Will to help us find appropriate candidates.....the soup kitchen is a perfect place to start, but from there, we can branch out all over the city..."

"I'm not going to be your supply boy," interrupted Will.

Remy waved his hand. "You're both just going to have to take some time to get used to the idea, that's all. It's all so new and different...."

Jane shook her head. "You have to stop this," she said.

"Jane's right," added John. "This needs to end now."

"No way," said Remy. "You're not going to ruin everything like you did last time!"

"Well, I think the robots are a great idea," said Ashley, giving her brother a supportive smile.

"Of course you do," said Remy, returning her smile. "You're a Crofton and a genius, just like me. We think and dream big, unlike the rest of the world!"

"So what do you say?" he continued, looking at Jane, Will, and John. "Are you in or out? It's your choice."

"There's no way I'm going to help you," replied Jane firmly.

162

"Oh no?" said Remy, with a dark smile.

"No," said Jane, "not in a million years. You don't know me if you think I'm going to take part in this."

"I actually do know you, Jane," he said, "better than you think."

Remy put his Brain Band back on and began interfacing with it. "And now for the pièce de résistance!" he said.

Suddenly, John, who had been sitting silently next to Jane, stood up stiffly.

"John here is going to provide us with a little entertainment too," said Remy, as he watched his friend stand up and walk across the room.

Jane reached for John's hand to pull him back onto the couch next to her, but he brushed her away.

"John," she said, "what are you doing? Why are you listening to him?"

"John, why don't you play us a song on the piano?" said Remy.

John walked slowly over to the piano and sat down.

"Something complicated, but maybe a little jazzy," laughed Remy.

John sat still for a moment, and then he put his fingers onto the keys and began playing a haunting, slow melody.

Jane stared at him in horror.

"What's wrong?" whispered Will.

"He doesn't play the piano," said Jane softly. "He's the most unmusical person I've ever met."

Jane looked from John to Remy, tears pricking her eyes. "How could you do this? To John!"

Remy laughed and replied, "I've improved him immensely, can't you see that?"

"But he's your best friend," protested Jane.

"Of course," said Remy, "but now that I have his brain scan, John is expendable."

"I like him better this way," said Ashley, with a giggle. "He's much more agreeable. He's going to make the perfect husband!"

"I think that's enough for now," said Remy. "Why don't you sit down again, John?"

Jane watched John walk stiffly across the room.

"So dearest Jane," said Remy, " if you help me, you can still save John. It's not too late. We haven't fried his brain yet. But if you don't help me, John is going to end up just like the man that you saw in the hallway last night. Now you don't want that, do you?

John sat down next to Jane on the couch, still under Remy's control.

"He doesn't know that you're controlling him," said Jane slowly. "Does he?"

"He has no idea!" laughed Remy. "Isn't it better that way?"

"Anyway, you and Will have until this evening to make your decision. We'll meet in the dining room for drinks before the party starts and you can let me know what you've decided. And remember, if you don't cooperate, John is no more."

00010111

DECISION

Jane and Will left the room in silence. Jane's head was spinning. She had assumed that Remy was up to something horrible. But never in her wildest dreams could she have imagined what he was actually doing.

"I should have known better," said Jane. "I know Remy. He wouldn't build my machine and then not use it. How could I have been so blind?"

"You can't blame yourself," said Will, gently. "What we need to do now is figure out how to stop him."

"And save John," said Jane, her voice shaking slightly.

"Of course," replied Will, "but we have to play our cards very carefully. If Remy was willing to turn John into a robot, he won't hesitate to do the same thing to us."

As they were speaking, John walked quickly out of the library. "I'm glad I caught you both!" he said, in his normal voice.

It was obvious that he was no longer under Remy's control and had no memory of what had happened.

"We have to stop Remy!" he said, urgently. "This is all so awful!"

"John," began Jane, softly, "there's something I think you need to know…."

Before Jane could say anything else, John interrupted eagerly. "Maybe I should talk to Ashley. She might be able to convince Remy to change his mind!"

"I don't think that's going to help…" said Jane.

"It might make a difference," replied John. "It's worth a try at least! Anyway, you don't know them like I do! She's the only one Remy listens to! I'll go talk to her. I know it will help!"

John hurried off, leaving Jane and Will alone in the hallway.

"Were you going to tell him?" asked Will.

"I thought I should," said Jane, "but maybe it doesn't matter at this point. We're going to have to figure out how to stop Remy without John's help."

"He really has no idea," sighed Will. "Plus, he has to be crazy if he thinks Ashley's going to help!"

"He's in love with her," said Jane. "It makes you blind, right?"

"Maybe...." said Will, looking at Jane meaningfully.

Jane looked at Will in disbelief. "This is no time for flirting!" she said.

"I know," said Will. "I couldn't resist! But I'm ready to be serious now...what are we going to do?"

"Don't worry," said Jane slowly, "I already have a plan."

"It better be a good one," said Will. "Or we'll be Remy's next robots."

***

"You two look stunning!" said Remy. He was standing in front of the sideboard in the dining room, mixing a drink. "Almost as good as me!"

"I'm glad that our earlier disagreement isn't going to ruin Ashley's birthday party," he added, taking a swig from his glass. "You know how much she loves all this stuff."

Will and Jane were dressed in costumes that Remy had provided for them.

"I'm not sure these outfits are really us," said Jane, looking down at the slinky beaded dress that she was wearing.

166

Ashely had chosen a 1920's theme for her birthday party and Will and Jane were both decked out in fashionable dress clothes of the time. Will was wearing a dark tuxedo with tails and a top hat, almost identical to Remy's attire.

"Oh try to have fun for once," said Remy. "Here, have a drink! It might help you to loosen up a little."

Remy mixed four more drinks, one each for Jane and Will, and two for himself. "Cheers!" he said, draining his glass.

Jane took a small sip and set her drink on the table.

"So," said Remy, expectantly, "have you come to a decision?"

"I don't think you've left us with much choice," said Will.

"Do you really expect us to let you destroy John?" asked Jane.

Remy laughed. "I'm not trying to destroy John, " he said. "But it does help to have some leverage."

"If I help you," began Jane, "I need guarantees. John's brain scan has to be completely…."

Just then, Ashley and John entered the room. Jane stopped speaking abruptly.

"Ooh!" squealed Ashley, as she caught sight of everyone's costumes. "We all look wonderful! Even you Jane!"

Remy smiled at his sister. "You look lovely this evening," he said.

"Of course I do," said Ashley, as she gave Remy a quick kiss on the lips in greeting. "I always look wonderful."

"Well," said Remy, "I'd like to have a toast, but first, let's get business out of the way, shall we?"

John looked over at Jane and shook his head silently. His discussion with Ashley had been a failure.

"You two are just in time," continued Remy, as he

walked back over to the bar. "Jane and Will were about to tell us their decision."

Remy turned and began mixing two more drinks. Ashley went over to him and draped herself over his shoulder.

"Yes," said Jane slowly, as she looked meaningfully at John. "We've come to a decision. We've decided to help you, Remy."

"You what?!" said John, shocked.

Jane walked over to John and stood next to him. "We don't have time for any more poking around," said Jane, giving John a gentle poke in the ribs as she spoke. "We'll help you, but we have a few conditions."

John looked at Jane, his eyes expressing his understanding. He nodded at her slightly.

"I told you they'd come around," said Ashley, triumphantly as she turned around to look at John. "Everyone does eventually!"

Remy turned and looked at Jane, a broad smile on his face. "And what are your conditions?"

"You know the first one already," said Jane. "But we do have a few more."

"If you help me," said Remy. "You'll be able to do anything you want!"

"Here's the deal," said Will. "I'll provide you with a certain number of subjects to turn into robots and Jane will get the machine working perfectly for you. After that, you're on your own. We never want to hear from you again."

Remy looked a bit surprised. "That's not a good business decision. You could be collecting profits for the rest of your lives if you continue working with me!"

"We know," said Jane. "But that doesn't matter. We want our lives to ourselves, and we want you to leave us alone."

"Alright," said Remy, reluctantly. "But I think you're

making a mistake. Why don't you think about it tonight? You might change your minds. Tomorrow, we can work out all of the details and make out a contract."

Jane nodded. "That's fine with us."

"And now John," said Remy, turning his attention to his friend. "It's down to you. What do you have to say for yourself?"

"Why not?," said John, looking directly at Jane as he spoke. "If Jane's on board, then I am too."

"Awesome!" said Remy, exultantly. "We're going to make the best team ever in the history of robotics! I can feel it. None of you will regret this! The three Amigas are back!"

"How about that toast you promised," said Ashley. "I think we have a lot to celebrate this evening!"

"Of course," said Remy. He held up his glass and said, "Here's to the beginning of a beautiful relationship!"

00011000

THE CHASE

It was very late when Jane and Will finally left Jane's bedroom. They could hear the sounds of the party coming from the floor below.

Jane adjusted her Brain Band and then gave an identical one to Will.

"I thought you left these in the room," groaned Will.

"I did," said Jane. "But the ones in the room are decoys. They'll buy us some time to get to the lab. These are the real ones."

"I hate Brain Bands!" muttered Will, as he lifted up his top hat to slip the brain band onto the back of his head. "They're worse than cell phones used to be. Plus they always give me headaches!"

"I know," said Jane. "They give me headaches too. But you need to wear this one. It's a key part of the plan."

"Fine," said Will, as he put it on. "But you're going to have to listen to me complain!"

"Don't worry," said Jane. "I'm used to it!"

Jane and Will crept to the edge of the stairway and looked over the railing at the party below.

"I can't believe the party's still going!" said Jane. "It's 3 o'clock in the morning."

Will looked at Jane and smiled. "That's nothing!" he answered. "Ashley's birthday parties are legendary. I wouldn't be surprised if it keeps going until tomorrow night!"

"I guess that helps," said Jane. "Hopefully everyone will be too drunk to notice us...especially Remy and Ashley!"

"Don't underestimate those two when they're drunk," said Will, as they made their way cautiously down the stairs. "I think it heightens their senses!"

Jane smiled ruefully. "You're probably right. So let's try to avoid them. There must be at least 200 people here. We should be able to get around without being seen."

"I hope so," said Will, as he led Jane down the stairs. "You know where we're going I hope?" he said.

"I do this time," said Jane. "I mapped the house on my Brain Band while you were napping. It was hard to concentrate because of your snoring, but I persevered. We shouldn't get lost this time."

"Sorry!," said Will. "One of my very few bad habits."

"Shhh," said Jane, as they reached the bottom of the stairs. "We have to get through the ball room and then we can cut through the kitchen to get to the back of the house. That's where the entrance to the lab is."

"We're still in these fabulous costumes," said Will, as he adjusted his top hat. "Let's try to blend."

As Jane and Will entered the ball room, they were overwhelmed by the crowd and noise. The room was packed with people and dance music was blaring. It was hard to make out anyone's features clearly in the dimly lit room.

"If we go quickly and don't do anything to attract attention, we should be fine," said Will.

Jane nodded and began to walk briskly across the room, making her way around the crowded dance floor. Will followed closely behind, looking back every so often to make sure no one was following them.

"Hey!" shouted a loud voice suddenly. "Stop! Where do you think you're going? Get back here!"

172

Jane and Will froze. It was Remy's voice. For a moment, they thought that he had seen them.

"What do you want, you naughty boy?" said a flirtatious voice.

A scantily clad blonde woman, who was a few feet ahead of them, turned around and walked back to the bar where Remy was stationed. As soon as the woman reached the bar, Remy put his arm around her and gave her a glass of something to drink.

"Phew," said Jane. "That was close. Luckily neither of us is Remy's type!"

"Did you see Ashley anywhere?" asked Will.

"No," said Jane, "but I wasn't really looking for her. She must be around here somewhere. It's her party, after all."

"Right," said Will, a trace of anxiety in his voice. "I'd just feel more comfortable knowing exactly where she was."

"Try not to worry," said Jane. "We don't have too much further to go. If we go through the kitchen we should be able to take the staff hallway from there all the way to the elevator that leads to the lab."

"And then what?" asked Will. "Didn't you say that we need Remy to get into the lab?"

"Yes and no," said Jane. "I'll explain when we get there. For now, let's just stay focused on getting to the lab before anyone notices that we aren't in our room sleeping. We don't have that much more time before my little Brain Band diversion won't work anymore."

Will nodded as he pushed open the door to the kitchen. As they entered the room, he gasped in astonishment.

There, before them, were about a dozen of Remy's staff members. They were all engaged in preparing food for the party, chopping and cooking busily.

"Let's get out of here," he said, edging back to the

door.

"It's okay," replied Jane cautiously. "I don't think they'll notice us."

Will looked at Jane incredulously and then looked back towards the workers. Although Jane and Will had been standing in the room for several moments, none of the staff had even looked in their direction.

"Why aren't they looking at us?" asked Will, nervously.

"Because they aren't programmed to," said Jane. "It's the way Remy's controlling them. I don't want to get into details, but the algorithms that he's using are very simple. The robots aren't able to do more than one thing, unless he changes the commands. Right now, they're only concerned with preparing food. We aren't part of that program, so they don't see us. Make sense?"

"Not really," said Will, who was eyeing the closest robot warily. The man was holding a large knife, with which he was rapidly chopping vegetables.

Jane and Will were about halfway across the huge kitchen, when suddenly all of the robots stopped their tasks. For a moment, it seemed as if they were frozen in place.

"Uh oh," said Jane.

"What do you mean, uh oh?" asked Will. "What's going on?"

"They're being reprogrammed!" said Jane. "Someone knows that we're here!"

Suddenly, the frozen robots began to move again. Almost as one, they turned towards Will and Jane. Perfectly coordinated, they began moving towards the couple.

"Run!" shouted Jane.

Jane and Will reached the rear doors of the kitchen only a few steps ahead of the hostile robots. They emerged into a large hallway that connected the kitchen with the rest of the house. Ahead of them, was a corridor that led to several store rooms.

"Are we in the right place?" asked Will, looking around anxiously.

"This is exactly where we want to be," replied Jane. "I just have to figure out…."

Suddenly, a loud voice interrupted Jane.

"Ha! I knew you were lying!"

Jane and Will looked up. There, ahead of them, blocking their way forward, was Ashley, surrounded by several humanoid robots.

"I told Remy that you would never willingly help him. God forbid that little Ms. Perfect does something bad!"

As Ashley spoke, the humanoid robots from the kitchen emerged from the door behind Jane and Will. They were surrounded.

"Your little trick didn't fool me for long!" said Ashley. "I was watching the fake feed from your Brain Band. Very clever…except for the romantic part with you and Will. That made me suspicious! I knew you were too much of a prude to do anything like that!"

"Wait? What were we doing?" asked Will.

Ashley looked around at the robots in satisfaction. "Anyway, it's over now and you're going to wish that you'd never tried to trick me or Remy. Plus, you're ruining my birthday party! That makes me even angrier. I don't like people who mess up my parties!"

Will looked at Jane and muttered, "You have a plan?"

"Of course," whispered Jane.

"Ashley, we're sorry for ruining your party," said Jane, with a slight smile. "We thought we'd make it up to you with a few parting gifts."

"What do you mean parting gifts?" snapped Ashley. "You're not going anywhere."

"Oh yes we are!" said Jane. She paused for a moment, interfacing with her Brain Band, and then said,

"Happy Birthday!"

As Jane spoke, alarms began blaring throughout the house. Lights were flashing on and off and several overhead sprinklers were activated, spraying water all over the place.

For a moment, the hallway where Jane and Will were standing was plunged into darkness.

"Come on," said Jane, grabbing Will by the arm. "We don't have much time!"

Jane and Will fled towards the storage corridor, making their way as best as they could in the semi-darkness.

In just a few moments, the entire party disintegrated into pandemonium. Costumed partygoers, disturbed by the alarms and flashing lights, were running all over the house. Some were panicked, trying to find a way out. Others seemed to be enjoying the show, assuming it was all part of the entertainment. Screams mingled with shouts of enjoyment. It was chaos!

"Quick," said Jane. "In here!"

Jane pulled Will into one of the store rooms that lined the hallway. She breathed a sigh of relief and, using her Brain Band, projected the unlit storage area into her visual field, thus illuminating the entire darkened room.

"What are we doing in here?" asked Will.

"This storage room should have a door in the back," said Jane, "It leads to a staff hallway, which is a shortcut to the elevator to the lab. It's a very old part of the house. I'm not sure Remy even knows about it, let alone ever uses it."

Jane looked towards the back of the room. There, just as she had said, obscured by a few old crates and boxes, was a door.

Jane walked over to the door and turned the knob. Nothing happened.

176

"Oh no!" she said, in dismay. "It's locked! And this isn't a computerized lock. It's an old fashioned one with a key. I can't do anything with this!"

The door was very solid, thick, and heavy. There was no way they could force it.

Jane began interfacing with her Brain Band, pulling up maps of the mansion. She scrolled through them rapidly, trying to find an alternate route to the lab.

"I think we're trapped!" she said nervously. "There's no other way to get there!"

"Ahem," said Will, trying to get Jane's attention.

"Not right now," said Jane impatiently, "I need to find another way to get the lab. We don't have much time."

"You don't need another way," said Will. "We can use this door."

Jane turned around sharply, "But it's locked…." she said, her voice trailing off.

Will was standing next to the opened door.

"How did you do that?" she asked, in bewilderment.

"Just because I'm not a computer nerd like you, doesn't mean I don't have any skills," said Will, ushering Jane through the door. "Being a reformed juvenile delinquent does have a few benefits!"

"I never thought I'd be happy about your former career as a criminal," said Jane, "but I guess it does come in handy every so often. We make a good team," she laughed.

"We certainly do!" said Will.

***

A few moments later, Jane and Will were at the end of the service corridor. The hallway, little used and forgotten, was dusty and filled with old furniture and cobwebs.

"They could use some housekeeping back here," said Will, brushing the dust from his arms. "Should I let Ashley know?"

Jane rolled her eyes and smiled. "Maybe later," she said. "Right now, we have more important things to worry about. This door should bring us to the lab entrance," said Jane. "There's an elevator that takes us underground and then we'll be almost there. If we can just get to the lab before Remy and Ashley, I think we'll be okay."

"Alright, lead the way!" said Will.

Jane and Will made their way cautiously across the room and towards the door that led to the elevator.

"I'm surprised there's no one here," said Jane. "Usually Remy has a few robots standing guard."

"They're probably all over the house dealing with the chaos you created," said Will. "And looking for us."

"I hope," said Jane. "I thought I'd have to reprogram a couple of the robots before we could get on the elevator, but that doesn't seem like it's going to be necessary. All I have to do now is override Remy's security precautions and we'll be in."

"Can you do that?" asked Will.

"I most certainly can," replied Jane with a smile. "You can pick physical locks and I can pick virtual ones. Plus, Remy's security is always much easier than you'd think. It's just like his personality. He's so arrogant...he doesn't think it's possible that anyone could outsmart him. He gets overconfident and sloppy with his code."

Jane interfaced with the security system, accessing several screens of code simultaneously. Within a moment, there was a familiar beeping sound as the access codes were accepted and the steel door in front of them slid open, revealing the elevator. As they entered the elevator, a computerized voice said, "Welcome Remy."

"The sound of success!" said Jane.

***

"Remy doesn't fool around when he builds a secret

lab," said Will, as they got off the tram.

"That's Remy for you," said Jane. "I think he likes the drama of it all. It's like we're in a sci-fi movie."

"I knew there was a reason I didn't like sci-fi movies," said Will.

The airlock closed behind them and the empty tram rushed back towards the mansion.

"Hurry," Jane said. "We don't have much time!"

Jane led the way across the outer chambers of the lab and towards the room where her machine was located.

The room was extremely still and quiet. It seemed as if they were the first ones there.

Jane sighed with relief. "We made it," she said. "I just have to do one thing and the machine will be useless."

"Great," said Will. "But hurry. I don't like it here!"

"I should be done in just a minute," said Jane, as she touched the machine on one of the access panels, tapping it gently a few times.

Suddenly a harsh voice broke the stillness.

"Not so fast! That's my machine now! Touch it again and you're dead!"

00011001

BUNNYKINS

Remy was standing in the center of the room, aiming a gun at Jane. Ashley and John were a few feet behind him. Ashley was smiling at her brother, while John had a pained look on his face.

"Hey," said Will, eyeing Remy warily. "I think we're letting things get a little out of hand. We're all friends here."

"Will's right," said John, anxiously. "We're all friends. I'm sure we can work something out."

"Friends!" said Remy. "Friends wouldn't do this to each other! This is betrayal!"

Jane looked at Remy, her face clouded with emotion.

"How can you talk about betrayal, after all that's happened between us?"

"What happened five years ago wasn't betrayal," scoffed Remy. "I have nothing to be ashamed of. But you do! You're preventing technology from advancing because of some silly moral code. You need to get over yourself, Jane!"

Jane's face turned red with anger. "No, Remy," she said firmly. "You're not going to use my machine ever again. I've made sure of that!"

"Ha!" laughed Remy. "That's what you think. I already checked the machine for any tricks that you might have programmed into it. You're too late!"

"And," continued Remy, "we have a little extra insurance. Show her Ashley!"

Ashley beamed with delight. She picked up a box and placed it on one of the lab tables. Then, she lifted a small, wriggling creature out of the box and set it down on the table.

Jane's face paled. "Bunnykins!" she whispered.

"Haha," laughed Ashley. "I never thought I'd get to say this, but I'm a bunny-napper! I took her out of your room while you and Will were gallivanting around the house. I thought I'd finally finish the job I started five years ago," she said, as she poked at the terrified rabbit on the table.

Remy laughed as he watched his sister torment Bunnykins.

"Johnny, dear," said Ashley, in her sweetest voice, "would you get me one of those scanners over there? I think this rabbit needs a good going over!"

"Ashley," John said, almost in a whisper. "Please don't. There's no reason you have to do this."

"Yes there is!" shouted Ashley angrily. "Don't worry... I'll get it myself."

Jane watched the scene unfolding before her with horror, paralyzed. She couldn't believe what was happening. It was just like five years before.

"I can't let this happen," said Will. He started to step forward, but Jane put her hand on his arm, checking him.

Jane took a deep breath. "No," she said firmly. "I have to fight this battle myself."

She took a few steps forward. Remy leveled his gun at her. "I will shoot you, Jane," he said.

"I don't care," she replied calmly, as she continued walking towards Ashley and Bunnykins. "I'm not going to let you use my machine to kill innocent people."

"Fine!" said Remy. "You asked for it!

Suddenly, before anyone knew what had happened, the gun had gone off and John, Will, and Remy were in a tangled heap on the floor, fighting.

"Finally, the men are acting like men!" said Ashley, with a satisfied sigh.

Then, she looked at Jane, and smiled sadistically. "Before I finish off Bunnykins, I have a little present for you!"

Ashley reached under the table and pulled out Robo-Bunny. "It's not as friendly as it used to be," she laughed.

"Sic 'em Robo-Bunny!" she cackled.

Jane looked in disdain at the robot rabbit as she walked towards Ashley. Just as it was about to latch onto her leg, she kicked it as hard as she could, sending it crashing into the back wall of the room. The robot jerked a few times and then went still.

Ashley gazed at Jane, speechless.

Without hesitating, Jane walked over to the table and punched Ashley squarely in the face.

"Nobody fucks with my bunny!" she seethed, to Ashley's crumpled form.

***

"It's too late," said Remy, a few moments later. "Like I said before, you can't stop things now. I disabled all of your little tricks. I'm in control of the machine. It doesn't matter what you do."

Jane, Will, and John had subdued Ashley and Remy. The two were tied up with some old electrical cord and pushed into a corner of the lab.

Will looked at Jane with concern. "Is that true?" he whispered to her.

"No," Jane shook her head softly. "You don't have to worry. Everything will be just fine."

Then she looked at Remy and said, "You really don't know me, Remy! Do you think I would trust you again?

"What are you talking about?" said Remy, a hint of anxiety in his voice.

"The Killer Poke! John and I were joking about it the other day in the lab," said Jane.

"What the hell is a Killer Poke?" said Remy.

"You really should have paid more attention in class," said Jane, shaking her head. "If you had, you might remember Professor Parsons' most famous quote: 'There is nothing that you can do that will irreversibly damage a computer…except a Killer Poke!'

Remy still looked blank. "Yeah, so….are you going to tell me what it is?"

Jane sighed. "It's a software command that tells a system to exceed the capabilities of its hardware. Usually, the command causes damage to the hardware. And normally, it's not programmed on purpose. But in this case, I did it intentionally. And it won't just cause a little damage. It will completely destroy the machine and the mainframe it's connected to."

"Have you seen the technology out there in the lab?" scoffed Remy. "I'm sure our systems can handle anything Plain Jane's brain might throw at them!"

"You're much too arrogant!" said Jane. "Computers seem so powerful and indestructible, but that's not always true. Sometimes, just pushing a few keys can destroy them. Professor Parsons taught us that every piece of hardware has an operational limit and a weak link. A system is only as strong as its weakest subsystem. The Commodore PET would destroy its own CRT monitor if you sent a BASIC POKE command to write a specific value in its I/O register. My machine, despite all of its advances, has a weak link too."

"I don't believe you," said Remy, angrily. "I think you're making all of this up! Why would you destroy your own machine? It doesn't make any sense!"

"Because of people like you," said Jane. "I never thought I'd have a reason to use a Killer Poke, until I designed my machine. I knew it needed some type of safeguard, so I purposely added a Killer Poke command into the design specs. You let the nanobots build the machine to my specs, without reviewing what they were actually doing. You might have noticed it, if you'd been paying attention. John saw it, but you didn't."

Remy looked at Jane in disbelief. "If you do this, you'll destroy all of your research too. Everything that you've done since you got here will be gone."

Jane paused for a moment and then said calmly, "I'm well aware of that. But it's already done. The cascade of failures has already been set in motion. When I touched the machine a few minutes ago, I activated the Killer Poke. And, as far as my own research is concerned, all that I need to complete my work is me. I may do it more slowly now, but I'd rather start all over again than continue using your tainted resources."

Jane paused for a moment, and then said, "So you see, Remy, it's not me that's too late . . . it's you."

Jane turned away and looked at Will. "Would you take care of them? Lock them in a closet or something. I don't want to have to deal with any more Croftons today. I'm going to check on John….he said he had to do some reprogramming to the lab security before we could leave safely."

Will nodded and walked over to Remy and Ashley.

"Alright," he said, pulling them up from the floor. "Off we go. I think this will do," he said, as he shoved them into a small side room off the lab."

"You should probably kill us," said Remy. "Just to be safe."

"Geez, Remy," said Will, as he started to push the door shut. "I'm not going to kill either of you! What's wrong with you?"

"He's right," said Ashley. "That's what we were going to do to you and Jane. It's the only smart thing to do."

"No killing," said Will, as he slammed the door shut.

"No matter how tempting it is!" he muttered to himself.

--

While Will was taking care of Ashley and Remy, Jane rushed over to John. He was seated in front of one of the lab interfaces, but he was hunched over strangely.

"John," said Jane, touching him on the shoulder, "is everything okay?"

John looked up vaguely. "Jane," he said weakly. "Sure, everything's fine. In a few more minutes it'll be safe for you to leave."

"You mean for us to leave," said Jane, looking at John more closely.

John turned slowly in the chair and grimaced. He moved his hand away from his side. It was red with blood.

"Remy didn't mean to shoot me," he said. "I think this bullet was meant for you."

"Oh John," said Jane. "I'm so sorry...."

"No . . . I'm sorry . . . about all of this," he replied. "How could I have been so blind? I should have known what Remy was up to. I think maybe I did know, but didn't want to admit it. Part of me has always wanted to be him...rich and confident and charming, all things that I've never been...."

John trailed off.

"John," said Jane, almost sobbing. "You've always been a thousand times better than Remy." She took his hand and held it tightly.

"I know Remy's been controlling me since the brain scan," continued John. "When I saw the look on your face after what happened in the library, I knew."

John paused for a moment, and then said, "At least there's one good thing that came out of all of this....I got a chance to see you again..."

Jane looked at him, but didn't say anything. Tears were rolling down her face.

John squeezed her hand and then said urgently, "Remy doesn't like to leave incriminating evidence behind. He has the entire lab rigged with explosives. Once those start going off, the nanobots are programmed to destroy everything in the lab, including themselves. Any interference with the mainframe computer initiates the program. Once you started the Killer Poke, the destruction sequence was started. There's no way to stop it. I did a few things that should help you. But you have to leave now, or it'll be too late."

"Please come with us" said Jane, desperately.

John shook his head. "This will be a good place for me to end. I always got along with computers better than people anyway."

Jane tried to smile, but failed.

"Here," he said, pressing something into her hand. "You might need this."

Jane looked at the small, wrapped item in her hand. "What is it?" she asked.

"A gift," he said, softly. "You'll see later."

Jane put her hand on his face and said, "Good bye, John."

"Never good bye," he whispered back. "Now go."

Jane turned away and walked across the lab to where Will was securing the door behind Remy and Ashley.

"We have to go," said Jane, trying to hide her tears. "The lab isn't going to last that much longer. Remy has some type of destruction program running."

Will looked at Jane and groaned. "Why doesn't that surprise me?"

"Where's John?" he asked, looking around.

Jane shook her head and looked away. "Remy shot him," she whispered.

"Oh no," said Will.

Suddenly there was a loud explosion behind them.

00011010

DESTRUCTION

Jane and Will ran out of the lab as explosions filled the air with smoke.

As they fled, Jane took one last look behind her. The entire lab was engulfed in flames. John hadn't been kidding. Remy wasn't leaving any evidence behind.

"What's going on?" panted Will. "Why did the lab just blow up?"

"Remy," breathed Jane. "He rigged the lab to destroy itself. He doesn't want anyone to know what he's been up to."

"Sounds like Remy," said Will, as he grabbed Jane's hand, pulling her forward, out of the lab and onto the tram platform.

"Not so fast!" said a loud voice.

Jane and Will stopped abruptly. Remy and Ashley were standing before them, blocking their way forward.

"You didn't really think you'd seen the last of us?" smirked Remy. "Remember, I'm the one who designed this entire complex. There are lots of secret ways in and out!"

"I told you that you should have killed us," giggled Ashley.

"Can't you see that it's over?" shouted Will. "Just let us go!"

"Let you go!" said Remy. "What kind of villain would I be if I just let you go?"

"Do you think that's a good idea, Ashley?" he asked,

turning towards his sister.

"Of course not," she said. "Plus, we have something for the two of you."

"Ah yes," said Remy. "Our final, parting gift, from us to you, with love!"

On the far side of the platform, all of the humanoid robots Remy had created, about 20 in all, were exiting the tram.

"They've been reprogrammed to dislike you!" he added with a sick laugh.

Jane looked at Remy and said, "What are you doing this for? You can stop this!"

"And spoil all the fun?" asked Remy. "Oh no! That would never do!"

"We hate to leave you here," he added, "but we'd like to get out of here before it's too late."

"Let's go Ashley," he said, taking his sister by the hand. "Good bye Jane and Will! It's been fun!"

As Jane and Will watched, Ashley and Remy ran towards the tram. They passed unmolested through the mass of robots, who didn't even register their presence.

In a matter of minutes, Remy and Ashley had entered the tram and sped away, leaving Will and Jane with no means of escape.

"Any great ideas?" asked Will, eyeing the advancing robots warily. "This is your field after all!"

Jane looked nervously at the robots. There was something about them that filled her with dread. They were human, but so inhuman at the same time. Remy had created a legion of monsters...the living dead!

"John said he'd try to help us get out of here," said Jane, hopefully. "Maybe he did something to the robots."

"It doesn't look like it!" said Will, as he watched them continue to advance, slowly getting closer and closer.

Jane looked behind her. The doorway to the lab was filled with flames and smoke. There was nowhere for them to go.

"I'll try to see if there's anything I can do," said Jane, interfacing frantically with her Brain Band. "Maybe John left us some clues."

"How about a less high tech solution?" said Will. He picked up a few rocks that lay near the entrance to the lab and hurled them at the robots, hitting one or two.

But it was no use, the robots kept advancing, their menacing gazes fixated on Jane and Will.

"There has to be something," said Jane, in desperation. Suddenly, she blurted out, "John…please help us!"

As Jane spoke, there was a bright flash and, as one, the robots all stopped in their tracks. They seemed to be at a loss as to what to do, trying to go forward and backward at the same time. It was as if they were listening to two competing programs.

"John figured out a way to reprogram them!" said Jane, in relief, as she watched the robots floundering.

"Thank you John!" breathed Will, taking Jane by the arm and pulling her past the robots. "Just in case it's only temporary, let's get out of here."

Jane looked back at the bewildered robots, her face creased with emotion. "We can't just leave them here. They look so lost."

Will's face looked pained. "I don't want to leave them either,"" he said. "But I don't think we have a choice."

Just then, there was another loud explosion, followed by a rush of smoke and flames from the lab entrance.

"We have to get out of here," said Will, taking Jane by the hand again. "We'll get help…and come back."

Jane nodded reluctantly, letting Will lead her away.

***

A moment later, Jane and Will were standing in front of the airlock doors that opened on to the tunnel and the tramway.

Will looked at the securely sealed doors in dismay. "Now what?" he said.

Jane scanned her hand on the scanner next to the door.

"Rejected," said a computer voice. The airlock door stayed firmly closed.

"What!" said Will. "What does that mean?"

"The airlock doors are only programmed to open if the tram is here," said Jane. "Normally I could override the commands, but it looks like Remy reprogrammed the airlock when he and Ashley escaped."

"So, fix it!" said Will. "You're much smarter than Remy. "

"Um," said Jane, nervously. "I'm not sure about this one...it's programmed differently...it's not like Remy at all."

Jane tried a few combinations, all of which produced the same negative result.

"What about John?" asked Will, suddenly. "He helped with Remy's robots. Maybe he reprogrammed Remy's password too!"

"You're right," replied Jane. She thought for a moment, and then began interfacing with the control panel.

"Approved," said the computer voice. "The door will open in approximately 10 seconds."

Will breathed a deep sigh of relief. "What did you do?" he asked.

"32 and 26," replied Jane, sadly.

"Your order at the restaurant!" said Will. "Of course!"

Before Jane could reply, the airlock door suddenly slid open. A sudden rush of air sucked them into the tunnel, knocking them off their feet.

Will got up and offered a hand to Jane. He dusted himself off and then looked down the length of the tunnel. "I guess Remy isn't going to send the tram back for us," he said, with an attempt at a smile. "Do you mind walking?"

"I don't think we have a choice," said Jane. "But I'm going to slow you down."

"I'd never leave you behind," said Will, taking hold of her hand again.

Suddenly, Will leaned forward and blurted out, awkwardly, "Can I kiss you?"

"What!" said Jane, in surprise. "Now? No! Don't you think we have more important things to worry about?"

"I don't know what else is going to happen. I'd never forgive myself if I missed my last chance to kiss you," replied Will. "At least give me something to hope for!"

"Alright," said Jane, with a small smile. "If we get to the other end of the tunnel in one piece, and if we make it out of the mansion and if…"

"Say no more!" interrupted Will. "We are definitely getting out of here safely!"

Suddenly, there was the sound of a massive explosion behind them. It was the largest one yet.

"Come on," said Will. "Run!"

Jane and Will ran along the tramway. The tunnel was filled with smoke, and they could feel the heat of the flames behind them.

"We need to go a little faster!" said Will, urging Jane along.

Suddenly, Jane stopped and her face turned pale. "Bunnykins!" she said, in a pained voice. "I left her in the lab. I have to go back!"

Jane turned around, heading back into the smoke and flames behind them.

"Jane," said Will, taking her firmly by the arm. "You can't go back. You'll be killed. Plus, it's too late anyway. Nothing could have survived that last explosion."

Jane felt her eyes fill with tears. She knew Will was right. It was too late.

--

After what seemed like an eternity, Jane and Will emerged from the tunnel, panting, coughing, filthy, and exhausted. The tram platform and the elevator that led to the mansion were in front of them.

"We made it," said Will. "Finally!"

Jane smiled slightly and then looked at Will. Tears began to roll down her face.

"We made it," she said, slowly. She was silent for a few moments before speaking again. "But it's hard to believe that we had to leave John and Bunnykins behind. I don't think I'll ever be able to forgive myself for forgetting Bunnykins."

Will smiled and removed his 1920's top hat, which had made it unscathed through their adventure in the tunnel.

He raised it up in the air dramatically and said, "Abracadabra!"

Jane looked at him, uncertainly. "Really Will, this is nothing to joke about."

Will reached into the hat and pulled out a small, fluffy rabbit.

"Bunnykins!" said Jane in amazement, not sure she could believe her eyes. "You saved her!"

He handed the bunny to Jane, who hugged her tightly.

"Thank you," she said to Will. And then, she leaned forward and kissed him.

00011011

RESOLUTION

Jane sighed as she put a few more books into a large packing box. She had already filled five boxes, and it still seemed as if her office was full.

"Maybe I'm more of a pack rat than I thought," said Jane, looking around the disorganized room.

Jane smiled as she saw Bunnykins hopping among her office debris. "It doesn't seem to bother you," she said to the rabbit, with a smile.

"I still can't believe we're leaving this place," said Jane to Bunnykins, as she pulled a poster off the wall. "I've been here for so long."

"That's why it's time to make a change," said a voice behind her.

Jane reddened, slightly embarrassed that she had been caught talking to her rabbit.

"Oh it's you Professor Chatham!" she said happily, as she turned around. "I didn't know you were going to be here today. I thought you were off with Will for the day."

"We got back early," he replied, settling down into a chair in Jane's office. "Apparently there's only so much baseball an old man like me can take."

Jane looked at him curiously. "What happened?" she asked.

"I got bored," he said, with a slight smile. "I forgot that I don't really like sports…it's been such a long time since I've been to a game. But it all worked out. Will didn't mind. We got to see part of the game and we had some vegan hot dogs together. It was a good bonding experience for us."

Jane laughed. "Well I'm glad it was okay."

"Everything seems to be okay lately," replied Professor Chatham. "I'm still not sure I believe everything that's happened in the past few weeks."

"I know," sighed Jane, perching on the edge of her desk. "It's hard for me to believe too, and I was there!"

"Will still hasn't finished telling me what happened after you got out of the lab," said Professor Chatham. "Every time he gets to that part he goes off on some tangent about how wonderful you are."

Jane blushed and looked away. "He's easily distracted," she said.

"But I think you're going to be disappointed," she continued. "There's not that much to tell. When we got back to the mansion, the police were already there. I guess all of the alarms that I set off triggered something and they sent a group of officers over to make sure everything was okay."

Jane smiled as she thought back to that night. "It was a crazy scene," she said. "People running all over the house in costume, the police swarming all over the place, me and Will looking like we'd just made it through World War III. It was chaos!"

"People are still talking about the party in town," smiled the professor. "I wish I 'd been there. It's being called the party of the century.

"Ashley always said she threw the best parties," said Jane. "In this case she wasn't exaggerating."

"Ashley and Remy," mused the professor. "They still haven't been found."

"No," said Jane, with a frown. "When we got back to the house, Will and I told the police everything. They were skeptical, but we kept telling them that there was

196

evidence in the lab. But, Remy's explosives caused the entrance to the lab to cave in. No one could get in until everything had been excavated."

"And when they finally did get in, there was nothing to be found," finished Professor Chatham.

"Because of the nanobots," sighed Jane. "They consumed everything! I thought there might be a little evidence left. But there was nothing! No evidence of my machine, no evidence of the humanoid robots, nothing! Just a burnt out shell underground."

"Remy was always very good at covering his tracks," said Professor Chatham. "I'm sure he had a plan from the beginning."

"I know," sighed Jane. "But it almost seems impossible that everything could have disappeared like that! There weren't even any bodies found…not the homeless men and not…"

Jane broke off and her voice wavered for a moment.

"John," said Professor Chatham softly. "It's hard to believe that he's really gone."

"I know," said Jane quietly, wiping away a few tears. "He was amazing. And he saved us. Whatever he did allowed us to get away."

"And he saved all of this," said Professor Chatham, making a wide gesture around the computer department. "I still can't believe that he gave all of his money away before he died…half of his fortune to his family, and the other half split between the university computer science department…and you…"

Jane smiled sadly. "He must have planned it for a long time. He always felt bad about what happened while he was here. He told me he was going to make it up someday."

"I think he did," said Professor Chatham. "I just wish he was still here with us to enjoy it."

"I know," said Jane softly, "I really do miss him."

"He left you quite a rich woman," said Professor Chatham.

"I still don't know that it's sunk in," said Jane. "Thinking about such a large amount of money...I've never had to do that before!"

"It will give you the freedom to do things you never thought were possible," said Professor Chatham. "I'm sad to see you go, but I know you'll be doing incredible work."

"I didn't think I'd ever be able to set up my own lab," said Jane. "It's going to be wonderful, but very strange at first. I'm so used to Malvern University. I'm going to miss this place."

"It's a good change for you, my dear," said Professor Chatham. "And don't worry, I'll still come see you. You aren't through with me yet."

Jane smiled, "That's good to know! I don't think research would be the same without you around to encourage me."

"And you're still dead set against trying to rebuild your machine?" he asked. "I know you lost the work you did in Remy's lab, but I still have all of the notes and files you shared with me."

"No," Jane shook her head gently. "At least not for quite some time. I think Remy taught me that we're not ready for a machine like mine. The brain is so complex. We don't understand all of the interconnections. Remy thought he did. And he used my machine to try to control people. But it didn't work. At least not the way it was supposed to. He killed innocent people!"

"I know," said Professor Chatham, gravely. "Perhaps we aren't ready for your machine in more ways than one. Until we can use technology wisely, it shouldn't be put into people's hands who are going to abuse it."

"You're right," said Jane. "But I'm not going to give up on my research. I just want to change my focus for a little while. When the world is ready for my machine, I'll be ready to rebuild it."

Professor Chatham looked at Jane and smiled. "That's what I like about you," he said. "You don't give up."

"I think I might have finally given up the past," said Jane, thoughtfully. "You were right about Remy. Facing him was something I had to do. I'm not the same person that was working quietly in the computer department a month ago."

"I know," said Professor Chatham. "It's clear to anyone who knows you."

Jane smiled, "I suppose I can thank Remy for that. He made me stronger."

"No," replied the professor, shaking his head. "You have you to thank for that. You made yourself stronger. I don't think we have anything to thank Remy for."

He paused for a moment, and then said, "I just wish that he wasn't going to get away with everything!"

Jane nodded in agreement. "I know," she said. "But there's absolutely no evidence. Once the police got into the lab, they must have thought the story that Will and I told them about humanoid robots was crazy! There was nothing there. They aren't even looking for Remy or Ashley. There's no reason why they should."

Professor Chatham looked thoughtful and then said, "I don't think we've seen the last of those two. They're not the kind that runs away and hides for very long."

"I know, said Jane. "But when Remy does come back, I'll be ready."

"Speaking of getting ready," said Professor Chatham, "don't you need to get going soon? Will said you two had a date tonight."

Jane looked at the time and started. "I didn't realize it was so late!" she said. Then, after a moment, she added, "It's not really a date….it's more like a get together...."

Professor Chatham laughed. "You can call it whatever you want, but I'm calling it a date!"

Jane, trying to change the subject, took a small, wrapped object off her desk.

"John gave me this," she said, "right before we had to leave him."

"What is it?" asked Professor Chatham, curiously.

Jane carefully peeled back the piece of paper covering John's parting gift. On the back of the paper, John had written the words 'FOR GOOD'."

In Jane's hand, was a nanobot.

STARGAZER BOOKS

Stargazer Books is a small publishing house with
big dreams . . . to find out more please visit

www.stargazerbooks.com

If you enjoyed this book and would like to help us
"spread the words" . . . please leave a review on

or LIKE and SHARE on

#ENCEPHALON

Look for other books by author Kerry Marie Sloan

https://amzn.to/2wtoxod

The Fountain of Death
(A Perfectly Silly Mystery)

Young Adult Fiction
for ages 11 and up

The Book of Westmere
First in The Guardian Series

Young Adult Fiction
for ages 11 and up

ATNAS
The South Pole Elf

Children's Book
Please read to your child

Look for upcoming books by author Kerry Marie Sloan

Witches Academy

The Guardian Series by author Kerry Marie Sloan

The Book of Westmere
The Four Towers

www.ingramcontent.com/pod-product-compliance
Lightning Source LLC
Chambersburg PA
CBHW070008260626
47159CB00005B/1720